The Doubtful Guests

Marion Douglas

The DOUBTFUL GUESTS

Marion Douglas

ORCA BOOK PUBLISHERS

First edition

Canadian Cataloguing in Publication Data
Douglas, Marion K. (Marion Kay), 1952-
The doubtful guests

ISBN 0-920501-92-3

I. Title
PS8557.O93D6 1993 C813'.54 C93-091119-9
PR9199.3.D69D6 1993

Publication assistance provided by The Canada Council

Cover design by Susan Fergusson
Cover painting "Mary" 1992, by David Goatley

Printed and bound in Canada

Orca Book Publishers
P.O. Box 5626, Station B
Victoria, BC Canada
V8R 6S4

FOR WENDY

Gayle

Lantau Island, Hong Kong – May, 1989

Can this be true? I am here already, on the other side of the earth, in this other century with Elizabeth. The flight must have been quite a bit faster than the speed of thought, because all of the worries and imaginings I left in Calgary do not seem to have caught up with me. Their poor little souls are most likely swimming across the Pacific now, whipping their tails, desperately trying to locate me so that they can stuff up my mind like a virus might. Or like the cotton Joel said they packed into his sinuses the time he had them scraped for polyps.

Well, they have not found me yet, so I am very pleasantly empty and everything in my environment has that rootless look of the unfamiliar. I fear that the six-foot cheffleras could be picked up and carted away at any time. And then I wonder where these mean and stealthy street dogs belong. Their ribs stand out and when they amble down the beach in packs they have the look of lines in a woodcut, wavering back and forth. New sights. Nothing rings memories. The daily staleness of old anticipations has been lifted and I wonder if this is perhaps what is meant by joy. Or is it only the principle of displacement brought to life? One thing pushed aside for another?

We were told in home economics class as we watched a wad of lard slipping about in a cup of water: this is how it works. And when the water was poured into the sink, the lard seemed to cling to the glass in a more repulsive and glistening way than it had before, prompting me to wish for the lard that it had never been involved in the displacement exercise at all. But I have been, and there is no undoing that, and the outcome will not be like the lard's, I hope. Things will get straightened out here. Although, already I am behind in what I should have accomplished. I have not yet written to Joel or Richard, and I have not yet fully explained to Elizabeth my reasons for being here. All of which weighs me down, but in a sodden and restful way, like the air in this place, making movement more difficult and anxiety slower in its approach.

I wonder if Richard has guessed where I have gone. It is not like me to surprise Richard, my only brother, my twin, but it really seemed best just to go. Joel would have wanted to talk and talk and analyze, and Richard would have said, "Just leave it be." But I can't. Even though Elizabeth knows less about that time than Richard, I believe she might know better, in a way that we do not, as if what she saw has been specially preserved, held perfectly still on a fresco. And then again, she may not. Whatever the outcome, it will be superior to secrets, which I have lost my taste for in all the clandestine planning of my getaway. I am convinced now that secrets must all be turned inside out like figs and exposed in a way that is not shameful, only too surprisingly and brightly organic.

Everything occurs gradually though, as Richard has so often said. What a temperate motto, and how like him. I suppose it is correct, everything does occur gradually, although interspersed with bursts of jet-speed activity to far-off airports filled with guards and guns and trapped humidity. One of my first impressions here was that it seemed as if the earth had inhaled all of its freshness, leaving nothing for us to breathe but secondhand air. As a botanist though, I think it good to undergo such changes in climate; it helps in the understanding of plant life, takes a person down to the vascular and lets her know what it can be like for the wordless varieties of life.

Elizabeth was there to meet me, thank God, with a car. "Welcome," she said. "You know what you are, of course, now that you're in Hong Kong. You're one of the guests, one of the doubtful guests. That's what my friend Charlie Reid calls us. Everyone's worried about what happens when the lease runs out. Not to ruin your welcome. Doesn't happen until 1997 anyway." And then she hugged me and grabbed my bags.

Our cousin has not changed as a result of her two years here. She had some very boring plans laid for me, including an immediate trip to the Chinese University to hear a talk on world hunger. "It will be interesting to you," she assured me, "data on arable land, wind and water erosion, encroaching deserts and so on."

I protested. "It's an unmanageable topic," I said, because I had no desire to go. My mind was jellied from fatigue, each step caused the people and their luggage to waver and the floor beneath my feet seemed to be giving like a suspension bridge. But, as is always the case, we went anyway, Elizabeth driving in first gear most of the way, arriving eventually at an auditorium filled with Anglicans. There were spiritual motives for the talk which surprised and affronted Elizabeth. I could not pay attention and slipped outside to stand in the breeze.

The heavy aroma of China was blowing out to sea, causing the bamboo to rub together with a porcelain clicking. I leaned close to the bougainvillea, seeking out its oxygen in the night and, as is the way with moving around the globe, my circadian rhythm was abruptly re-established and my mind was as if placed, wide awake, on a sunny roadside in Alberta. I might as well have been driving south to collect weeds, with Joel coming along for the drive, worrying about some aspect of his body's functioning and searching for a better cup of coffee in each of the small towns we would pass through.

I imagined him sitting in our house with the flowers I left him and that note, that weak and inadequate note. I could see him thinking the most unlikely reasons for me being here, chasing after the least likely contingency, just like Reba would, hunting it down on a river bank to find that it is only a stick or a rock. What would he be saying to himself, I asked, but did not answer.

Elizabeth left the talk early and we drove back into the city to the ferry terminal. The car was not hers, it had been borrowed from her friend Charlie – possessions here are less possessed than in North America – and it was entertaining to watch her struggle with a standard transmission. It is ironic that one as practical as Elizabeth has never learned how a gear shift works. The engine, so often stuck in first as it was, and wailing for change, reminded me of how I felt before leaving Calgary, and out of sympathy for it I repeatedly said, "Push in the clutch and I'll shift."

But, "No," Elizabeth would say, waving a cigarette dismissively, "it's doing just fine." Smoke was coming from the hood and the heat gauge was pointing to the red zone by the time we arrived at the ferry.

Who was it who used to say, "Elizabeth, she's such a brick!"? I think it was Aunt Jean and I think I understand now what she meant. Elizabeth is immutable. She travels from place to place with firm resolve, just as her jaw would suggest. Not the rip-snorting type of resolve or the contemptuous sort or even that of the optimistic bon vivant. She simply builds a campsite for herself and then strikes out, finds work and learns the language, but always in her wardrobe of relics and with her reel-to-reel set up in the bedroom. It's that she concludes each day with a message on the tape recorder that makes her a constant to me, that makes her a brick. Joel told me once, at a time when a muscle in his left thigh twitched off and on for a month, that he could not imagine Elizabeth experiencing a nervous tic. (I think it was the period when Joel was completing his thesis work and Dr. Hoffman had suggested that perhaps "erudition exceeded his grasp.") At any rate, I concur with Joel's assessment. She is never too tired, too anxious, or too premenstrual to turn on that reel-to-reel and make some observation about the day.

This is all meant to say that Elizabeth is unchanged, except that she keeps her red hair tied back in a knot so that it is off her freckled neck. She is studying Mandarin and consorting with communists. On the ferry she spoke to some men in variegated sounds which they appeared to understand, and watched knowledgeably as they played mah-jong, the game which goes on every night in the restaurant below us. The stirring of the tiles gives off a noise reminiscent of menacing insects. Then there are the sharp knockings as the tiles strike the table.

Elizabeth is sharing this apartment with a woman whose name is Miranda. Miranda has two children, Jocelyn and Willy. Willy has a head that looks very hard, harder than normal, and is bullet shaped and when he runs, this bullet shaped head leans forward and tows him along. Jocelyn has purplish circles under her dark brown eyes. Her skin looks very, very soft, like the petals of a marshy, shade-loving plant. There is an estranged husband and father living in Hong Kong and practising dentistry. According to Miranda it was this husband, Gordon, who insisted that the family move here from Australia five years ago because he wanted to live on an island that was not continent-sized.

Miranda has a loom which fills what is called the living room. She weaves with thin strands of cotton, blue and white, black and white, grey and white, always human figures running in a geometric way. She has told me that weaving brings on migraine headaches for her so she must be careful to keep track of all sorts of cycles before sitting down to weave – the moon's fullness, which hormones are waxing or waning within her and the movement of the ocean and the stars. It seems as if the entire universe must relax its grip on Miranda before weaving can be undertaken.

The walls of the living room have been decorated by the children with stamps from South America and India and many other distant ports of call from which Miranda's departed lovers write. And Elizabeth tells me there have been many more of them.

It is only five in the afternoon as I write this and I am tired, not having fully adjusted to this place. And last night I awoke at 3:00 a.m., brilliantly wide awake, as if floodlights had been switched on in my room. I was filled with energy and in the mood for arranging things, picking them up and setting them down again and moving my few Pepsi crates, the only furniture in my bedroom, here and there. I wandered to the living room – nothing to do there – so I proceeded to the bathroom, closed the door and began examining and cleaning.

Jocelyn is a strange little girl. She keeps a plastic bag in the bathroom in which she stores her own roll of toilet paper, soap, bits of paper and pencil crayons and a wadded facecloth. The toilet paper is usually soggy, but less so than the other roll because there is no shower stall, only a nozzle which sprays everything before the water drains through a mouse hole opening in a corner of the room. This is why I use Jocelyn's paper, even though I know enough about her to suspect that an intimate reason probably exists for this separate supply. When I enter her private bag of goods I feel as if I am committing a disgraceful act, like the time I opened Joel's journal and read an entire page before slamming it shut and replacing it on his desk just so.

After the bathroom, I stood in the living room again, wakefully awaiting morning in Asia, leaning against the loom. Leclerc, it said on it, from Quebec. Strange to have this large manufactured product from Canada here. As I stood there I remembered a time when I still believed that Dad may have wandered off to the Gaspé, may have been incarcerated in an asylum called Tranquille or Serenité. It was possible, after all; he may have become irreversibly insane. When we were nineteen, my friend Helen and I drove along the St. Lawrence to the ocean, just in case, although only I knew the reason, stopping for loaves of bread baked in outdoor ovens, always an expectation in my stomach, an unusual excitement, "that extra category of life," as Dad used to call it.

Perhaps I was a little homesick last night because the stamps on the wall set me thinking of home also, and the evenings spent with the Majestic Stamp Album. There were those times when Dad had an unaccountable need to fill every space on a specific page in that book. "What the hell difference does it make?" Mom would ask, and he would say, "I just like it to be complete."

I remembered the day we drove to Toronto with Elizabeth to see Aunt Peg at the cancer hospital: Aunt Peg growing downward into her bed and folding in upon herself like a calyx in the fall, changing colours in unexpected ways. We stayed and talked and, as usual, "her spirits were good" even though her voice sounded as if it were calling from some spot barely above the earth's surface. And when we left, Dad said, "There's a stamp store near here. I looked it up in a telephone book in the library." He so often would surprise us with this type of information, denoting a life of searching that went on, unbeknownst to us, in phone booths and libraries and town offices.

We tramped along the streets looking rural, no doubt, possibly like recently arrived immigrants, with uncertainty in our gait and too much circumspect watching of cars and buses as if they might leave their streets and chase us down. We found the shop easily; "Phabius Philatelist" it was called.

Phabius was small and pale with wavy black hair and a cigarette burning in a rectangular ashtray which had scalloped edges, like a stamp, I remember thinking. Dad began talking, a streak of words, about Albania and King Zog and the single empty space on our album's page where a stamp from Albania was intended to be. "Although there is no likeness, no picture," he said, "we presume it would be for the face of Emperor Hoxha who discredited Zog for his alliances with Greek dancing girls and the like – we've read up on the situation some – so, presumably there would be very little in circulation bearing the face of King Zog. My children certainly prefer emperors to kings, however, so if you could kindly direct me to your Albanian section or drawer, file or what have you." Dad often used to finish his flourishes of talk with a group of synonyms, as a way of slowing down or emptying whatever cup of thoughts he was pouring forth.

Phabius started upward while Dad spoke, as if his words were bats beating their wings throughout his shop. He seemed not to like Dad, or perhaps any of us. Then, looking at my father, he said, "I have nothing for you."

What was most memorable about Phabius was his immobility; only his lips parted, to speak. The cigarette was not touched and his hands lay somewhere beneath the counter. I recalled believing that between his white thumb and his gently crooked forefinger, he was holding the one Albanian stamp known to exist in all of North America. Back then I often felt that people were trying to dupe Dad or cause him to appear foolish.

Dad said, "So be it. We can get everything else we need through the mail. It's only Albania that's given us any trouble."

Phabius looked at his cigarette ash and we left.

Outside it was raining and mother said, "Well, Duncan," which was her way of wondering aloud, I think, forcing a pause in the endless speech of living, for she never concluded this opening. There is no telling what she was thinking; it could have had to do with the rich and the poor, or affectation, or time better spent elsewhere. She never directly commented on Dad's behaviour, his excessively detailed talk, his days of animation and his days of silence, his driving here and there, his restless need to complete this or that silly project, and his swimming. As a result, we did not wait for a sequel; instead, we ran. Leaves fell like wet little hands and clung to us but we ran on, a brigade of country folk, to the Pontiac.

Darkness fell before we were far from Toronto and mother insisted on having the interior light on so that she could read. It must have been that, driving along in a tin bauble of light, that caused a vague feeling of separateness to set in for me that night. I recall it so well, the five of us absconding with a bit of city brightness to the then quiet southern Ontario fields. "The amphibians have all dug out now for the summer," Elizabeth said when we arrived home. The car's interior light was turned off, as were the headlights, likewise the yard light. Still, I had a knowledge of something after that day which I realize now; maybe that Dad was more than a little different, or maybe that as a family we were like the illuminated passengers in a car at night, needlessly visible.

I did finally fall asleep last night, the jet-lag alertness left me, and now I must force myself to stay awake. Miranda will return soon from her secretarial job and Elizabeth will come later, on the last ferry. The classes she teaches are all in the evening. Until Miranda arrives, I may go for a walk in the hills with my taxonomic guide and study the plant life and struggle with my drooping eyelids.

The earth seems older here, and there are pathways everywhere, deep and well-used ruts, the kind the cattle made in Ontario. And the most startling sights. In Calgary everything seemed to have been placed, sensibly, in rooms, or arranged in some fashion as if large and practical florists had been at work at night. Here there are odd tableaux which cause me to swoon almost, temples in the forest and old men in black suits drinking tea on the beach at night. Next door, people spray-paint bags that appear to be made of canvas or vinyl, a luminescent orange. They hang from bamboo racks in our neighbour's yard, which is in reality an outdoor factory. By day, women sit at tables and sew the mysterious bags which are baled and loaded on to dollies for shipment, carcass-like in their emptiness. The eyes are entranced with these new sights and I wonder why I have not travelled more in my thirty-four years.

On second thought, I will not go outdoors. I will stay inside and try for a feeling of missing Joel. I plan to buy some underwear for him and some T-shirts to dye; he is the one who taught me how to dye. The underwear will have been made in China, Double Happiness brand. Joel will enjoy the lettering and the joviality of the packaging. Tomorrow, or at least very soon, I will send these things with a long letter, explaining everything.

I can see Miranda coming now from the ferry, so I will begin to prepare the fish soup. She is wearing her large and perhaps ridiculous straw hat. People make fun of her and I am not sure why. I am never certain about the ridiculous and the not so ridiculous; I have always had to watch for others' reactions to know exactly what to think.

Richard

Calgary

"Well," Richard thought, hanging up the phone, "I figured she was in Hong Kong." He was relieved though, to know for certain – Gayle had called Joel and let him know, just as Richard had predicted. And now Joel was on his way over with more details.

"Phew," Richard said, sitting down with his newspaper. And then again, "Phew." He did not like this taking off behaviour of his sister's. On the two previous occasions when she had disappeared she had told him her plans; not this time, however. And that had scared him. His heart was still pounding in his ears as he thought, "I'm getting too old for this type of thing. Way too old, I don't like it one bit."

Then again, having begun scanning the newspaper, Richard corrected himself, thinking no, that's not true. This is actually the sort of thing I do like. At least in print. The baffling. The inexplicable.

The stray event. And pausing, looking up, he said aloud, "The Briefly," then looked down again and began to read.

Richard could not remember a time when newspapers had been unimportant to him, which was odd, he knew, because foreign affairs, budget speeches, labour news, the Middle East and so on had never really interested him. He had subscribed to the *Manchester Guardian Weekly* for a while but had soon let it lapse because incisive commentary and analysis were not what Richard sought. Instead, he purchased two or three papers daily, leafing quickly to the inside pages to sections labelled "Briefly" or "At A Glance," or searched for the small and tragic reports tucked beneath ads for LSAT study courses or weight-loss programmes. "Little League Game Ends in Tragedy," he had read today and clipped out, and yesterday, "Swamp Lady Dies."

These jarring little pieces aroused in Richard a contemplative mood, as if someone had thrown a bucket of water onto a marble floor, leaving him to observe the errant flow of liquid. And so he would sit, imagining details which only served to convince Richard that we, people in general, were not necessarily the maze-brightest rats to which Joel occasionally made reference. Like the dimmer rats, Richard's "Brieflies" and "At A Glances" seemed to prove, people often got lost on the way to the cheese, barreled down the wrong passageway or stood for disqualifying periods of time sniffing an unknown substance beyond the barrier.

Richard muttered to himself, "Take the swamp lady as a case in point," leading a cranky and eccentric existence which, these days, appealed to him. She had probably lived alone for years, lighting her cabin with dozens of devotional candles, eating birds' eggs and walking the woods with a runny-eyed dog. Groups of young boys had probably terrorized her, thrown foetal pigs at her door, stolen from the veterinary college, perhaps. Richard invented and imagined these indignities in his living room, then wondered what had held this woman at such a distance from humanity for so many years and why she had been tormented for this choice.

There were occasions when Richard's wanting to know certain details became so passionate that he would call directory assistance and seek out the telephone numbers of individuals mentioned in the paper, anyone with the same surname, thinking that he might call someday. Afterward, he would usually lie down, feeling nauseous from a sense of having gone too far, or pick up the paper to read another, more benign piece, so as to return himself to a more neutral state of mind.

The Little League game tragedy was one such piece, for it at least had a point of negligence from which to assign responsibility. The mother had driven through a red light. But, what had distracted her? Richard wondered. Had she had her hair cut and did it look too boyish? Was she examining it in the rearview mirror when the crash occurred? Richard would stand by his stove waiting for the kettle to boil or sit and sharpen a pencil, puzzling over such details. Before Gayle left, this business of the "Brieflies" and the "At A Glances" had been merely an interest, albeit a somewhat private one, as he had never confessed to anyone about the phone calls. But now, with Gayle gone and a noticeable surplus of hours in the day for him, Richard worried that his interest might be becoming a preoccupation. With all this extra time he could even worry about his worrying.

It was not only the newspapers. Without Gayle to call or meet for walks, Richard had begun, it seemed to him, to encourage his mind to locate and follow the narrowest strands of thought, but to no useful end whatsoever. Tonight, for example, the last evening in May, Richard had passed a good half-hour considering that the drive-in movies would be open with their silent, monolithic screens and that maybe a restless farmer would lean upon a fence in the nearby countryside and watch the enlarged blue-green faces of extra-terrestrials moving against the sky. He wanted this man to watch the movie with no understanding of its plot, but to return to his home feeling gainfully entertained, nevertheless.

Richard was concerned that he was spending too much time in unproductive thinking; he believed that he was spending far too much time pacing and looking out of windows. He wished that he could feel more at ease in his own home and even went so far as to write this intention down. "Try to feel more at ease in your own home," Richard printed on the back of an envelope. He laid down the pencil and concluded that he was likely the only person north of the Bow River who did not own a fridge magnet. Having to tape the envelope to his refrigerator was, he thought, just a small measure, just a tiny confirmation, of the fact that he inhabited a margin few others shared. This margin had not seemed so apparent to him before Gayle left, just eight days ago.

The street lights blinked on with their electronic uniformity and Richard began to wonder, with some irritation, about the brightness of his own sister, bustling away within her maze, moving inward but getting no closer to the cheese. Richard imagined her running past thickets, hedges and topiary, the top of her head barely visible to those left standing there at home, puzzled as to why she had taken that particular route and worried that she would come up against impenetrable walls of thorn, appearing "At A Glance" in the *Calgary Herald* within a month or two.

So many people's lives had often seemed an inscrutable series of acts to Richard; he was used to that. But not Gayle's surely, he thought; it should be different with one's own twin sister. Her life should be as clear as a coloured map, with plans, motives and all desires coded like explorers' routes. He would certainly not have done such a thing; he would never have had such a far-off and impulsive voyage charted on his map. Then Richard thought for a moment of how a cartographer would portray his movement around Calgary: dark brown ruts between his apartment and the university library where he worked, a grey rut between his house and Gayle and Joel's house, and a greenish rut to Sandra's duplex. None of these dotted lines all over the globe. Although, he admitted, there had not been that many trips for Gayle. South America, after Mark and before Joel. England, after Tony and before Mark.

"I don't know why I keep expecting us to be similar—you'd think I'd have given up on that fantasy." Richard thought to himself, "We have no more in common than any other pair of siblings. Just because we shared the same amniotic fluid . . . The old ladies at the church were maybe right after all."

And with a smirk, Richard asked, of no one, in a falsetto voice, "Are you sure you two are related? I think the storks flew in from two different countries. Gayle's as dark as Richard is fair."

Yes, Gayle was dark, like their father, Duncan McDonagh, had been. Her hair fell in heavy, black waves and when adolescence arrived, her eyebrows thickened and Gayle debated with Richard whether to pluck them or shave them off entirely. She decided upon the latter and then never got around to painting on the Elizabeth Taylor-like brows she had pictured herself wearing. For that period of time, when she had lived completely without eyebrows, Gayle had had the perplexed yet manifest look of a character from one of the Doctor Seuss books. Years later, that expression was what Richard still saw when he watched her face closely, moving, as we all do, from cupboard, to window, to Reba, her dog of many years.

As for Richard, his hair was still very blond and his eyes blue, the sort of blue that had caused the residents of their home town, Unity, Ontario, to look again and comment, the sort of blue that is both charming and persuasive. It had been only the day before that Richard realized his interest in the random, the brief, the at a glance, had arisen as a direct result of his blue eyes.

The winter he was nine, the winter of 1965, one of the ladies in the church choir pointed out the similarity between his and Elaine Wheeler's eyes. "Look at this, will you," Mary Ellen Ford had remarked in the church vestibule, pulling Elaine and Richard together for comparison. "Such an unusual shade. Reminds me of the western bluebirds I saw out in Regina last summer." It became a point of interest that no other individuals in or around Unity had eyes the shade of blue that Richard McDonagh and Elaine Wheeler, church organist, possessed.

"Perhaps," Richard had reasoned at that time, "Elaine is actually my mother." He remembered thinking it a convincing bit of chicanery, this telling him and Gayle that they were twins. How else to explain the closeness in age? Was it his or Gayle's actual birth date that was celebrated, he wondered, along with a host of other details which interested him in a detached and empirical way.

There were two ideas, however, which Richard did ponder at length and with some feeling during that time. The first was: what was there to stop him from simply going home to Elaine's house one day after school? If he did that, wordlessly sat down at her table, moved into the rhythm of her evenings teaching piano, would it matter? It had seemed to Richard that it would make as much sense as his presence in his own home where he often felt he had arrived by mistake, or by taxi. Richard smiled to himself when he recalled his childhood belief of having been delivered by cab, having stepped out, at the age of four or five, from its back seat.

The second question Richard used to ask himself as he followed Elaine's nails up and down the white organ keys was: had she, before deciding to do the right thing and give Richard up to his father, ever changed his diaper?

It was in the summer, when Elaine began to bring recordings of black gospel music to the church, exhorting the children's choir to raise their arms in acts of praise (which they did do, compliantly and shamefacedly), that Richard judged Elaine to be much too tempestuous to have borne him, the cautious one, the one whose heart filled in a most satisfying way when he had finished making and decorating book covers from paper bags for all of his school texts at the beginning of the school year.

Altogether, he had supposed eventually, he was more suited to his own family, even though Gayle and Duncan had most often seemed to be flying in a lunatic twosome, the way cabbage moths will, and Louise, his mother, was usually seen driving in and out of the laneway in various cars and tweedish suits and authoritative hats. Richard had kept a couple of those hats after Louise died and he still occasionally took them out and admired their cut and the black felt of which they were made.

Richard recalled observing them, the hats, and all of the other movement of people and clothing in their household, from the vantage point of a number of farm vehicles and windows; he had been a watcher for as long as his memory stretched. His bedroom window was the preferred observation deck, especially during winter, after the skating rink had been made. Every December Duncan had made a skating rink for the kids, stringing Christmas lights around it on snowfence. Children from other farms, and even a few of the town kids, used to come and skate in the evening. Gayle had a crotchety Sea Breeze record player in a white vinyl case that was placed on a stool at the end of the rink, attached by myriads of extension cords to an outlet in the basement. They played stacks of forty-fives by the Supremes and the Four Tops. Frequently, Louise would drive in from a meeting and, turning into the driveway, the arching headlights would brighten the children's clothing briefly, causing reds and yellows and greens to appear against their sudden shadows.

Duncan rarely skated on the rink with the children. He was an insomniac and would often go out to the ice in the middle of the night, awakening Richard or Gayle with that pleasing sound of metal on ice, the same glassy rasping heard when frost is scraped from car windows. Once, deep in winter, Richard had looked from his bedroom window to see Gayle walking toward the rink on her toes, as girls in figure skates do. She wore a red jacket and white hat and the way she propelled herself along the icy path seemed to be like the yearning she had for her father, a running after on tiptoes, a stumbling headlong. And when she reached the ice and skated toward Duncan's arms, Richard heard, "You've come to skate with me, have you, my favourite little girl child." Richard remembered that Gayle was wearing plaid slacks beneath her nightgown. They had held hands and skated round and round among the Christmas lights.

It was because of his watchfulness that Richard had often appeared to be aloof, and this aloofness had at times been called stand-offishness. The community's opinions were all altered, however, one summer five years after Duncan had left, when Richard pulled a dying girl from Lake Huron, reviving her with mouth-to-mouth resuscitation. His picture appeared in the *Unity Informer* and people began to speculate that he might turn out to be like his mother, who was "active." That had been during Richard's final month of high school, and to this day he still remembered the feeling of relief as the drowning body took its first rattling breath, not so much because she had been returned to life, but because he knew, with a gratitude that only the temperamentally lazy can appreciate, that this was all he ever need do. Since that day, Richard had not tried, really hard, at anything. To exert one's self would be to overdo it, he believed. Still, the end of each day brought him a sense of intense completion, in the way a day of camping will.

Looking out of his kitchen window for Joel who was due to arrive soon, Richard was thinking tonight, though, about beginnings. This time Gayle's disappearance had been a little bit too much like their father's—no warning, no explanation. Richard saw them now as the two loops of a strangely knotted bow. And along with all the other pointless brooding he had done since Gayle's leaving, Richard had spent a considerable amount of time wondering where this had all begun. He wished that he had saved those United Breeders calendars that had hung above the telephone every year of his childhood. There might have been a day circled back then by their circumspect mother, indicating the first time Duncan had gone off.

That had been Louise's expression for it, "off." She had a penchant for choosing the most correct word, the simple hackneyed phrase and rendering it apt so that people listened anew. "He was off then," she would say, referring to a period of time she would not exactly have forgotten or discounted but placed slightly beyond the capable vocabulary of her mind. Louise seemed to think of Duncan's odd phases in electrical terms. He was off; he had been switched off like an appliance, or was otherwise malfunctioning. Images of faulty vacuum tubes in their old G.E. radio probably entered her mind from time to time.

It never ceased to amaze Louise McDonagh that there were days when her husband could not put himself to work. She could have brought organization to a snow storm; at least, that is what Phil Hansen said in an address to the Rotary Club one blustery night. The occasion had been the presentation of a plaque in appreciation of the work Louise had done for the exchange student programme. Several students had come to Unity, from Finland, and several local students had gone there. The speaker's series at the Elk's Hall had been her idea as well; Richard and Gayle had helped to stencil the posters that had read, "Concerning the Nuclear Threat."

There had always been an issue: school legislation, marketing boards, by-law changes and so on. It seemed to Richard now that the many disparate components of any occasion – tables and chairs, coffee urns, agendas and executives – must have been attracted into place by Louise in a manner as subtle as gravity or magnetism. If only she could have had the same effect on domestic situations, Richard thought.

Richard took heart from the fact that his parents had hosted parties, though, during the good times when Duncan was not off, not planning to swim to Bay City, Michigan, or complaining that his hands could not write a cheque properly. Richard had always taken heart from those parties, which testified to something sentimental in Louise's character and the rare and tenuous love she felt for Duncan. On party evenings, neighbours would arrive, card tables would be set up and the gin and rye bottles placed on the battered arborite countertop. Trumpets and saxophones played on the stereo, and often Duncan and Louise were the only ones who danced.

Watching their place from above, Richard thought, an audience would have seen times when cars drove the long laneway frequently, parking themselves close to the maple tree, as if they were cattle, and other times when the square brick house stood alone, a singular planet, the yard light casting such abrupt perimeters it would seem a person could fall off into the surrounding darkness. "The point is," Richard said out loud, "the point is, people did come and go." It's not as if we were like the Bishops, he thought, our pale and isolated and probably consanguineous neighbours. Surely my life will not turn out like Angie Bishop's, he thought, genetically unfortunate from the start and concluding with mysterious hospitalizations for undiagnosable nervous problems.

What a jangled pile of nerves is time, Richard thought. So long ago it all was, more than twenty years in fact, long enough to accumulate a pile of nerves so knotted and tangled no comb, no matter how fine-toothed, could unravel them. To think that he could find a day on a calendar, a white rectangle with black numerals from which to cast out lines, straight and possibly biblical in design. This was not possible. It was a case of Duncan and Louise begat Gayle and Richard who in turn begat only unproductive motion through life, such as unexplained trips to Hong Kong and obsessional clipping of newspaper items.

Joel had told Richard once that when he was a boy a wood tick had attached itself to his neck and when his mother pulled it away there had been a tenacious sound of clinging and tearing. He said that he thought it was like the sound of a memory being torn out of hiding and into sight. And as Richard thought about this whole business of tweezing out memories he wondered if perhaps they would be better off left embedded in the skin.

There was Joel now, pulling up in front, trying to parallel park on a busy Memorial Drive. He was still driving his rusty Fiat; he was still not able to parallel park without driving a rear tire on to the curb and thumping down again to the street.

Richard liked Joel. He had a world-weariness about him, Richard believed, because of his mental health clinic work. He had seen too much of the street-dwelling type of deviance, the people who were different even on the surface, with hair that was impossible to alter from its slept upon flatness or skin too cratered to be of this planet. Richard liked Joel's habit of reducing events to the physiological. Joel claimed to be able to imagine neurotransmitters gushing from pale blue sacks in the midbrain when a person appeared to be too happy, or electrical forks like lightning drawing close to a cell, then missing by a hair's breadth when a person had the sense of a word or a name on the end of his tongue. But the flipside of this was an annoying hypochondriasis. Joel spent too much time visualizing his lungs, his kidneys, the Heimlich manoeuvre. Just the thought of choking made his hands sweat, he would say.

It seemed to Richard that all of Joel's consideration of the inner and the cellular had made it more poignant that he had had no awareness, not the slightest premonition, of Gayle's plan to leave. All that Richard knew was that when Joel came home from work on the day of Gayle's departure, there had been a vase of thirty-six tulips on the coffee table and a dozen brassy peonies on the kitchen table, all taken from the botanic garden where she worked. The accompanying note read, "Dear Joel – I have gone away for a spell. I need to. Will call soon. Give Reba to Richard if she's too much trouble. Love, Gayle."

Joel had instantly telephoned Richard. It was shabby, yes, Richard agreed that it was shabby. He had said so repeatedly, while Reba barked and barked in the background.

And Joel had said, "I feel as if some very small mechanics entered my brain and did a bit of work while I was eating lunch today. None of the old connections are working, and it was all done when I wasn't paying attention, like when someone pulls the spark plugs from your car then sits behind a shrub, watching you try to start it. It's a big laugh. I mean, a lot of people must have known – all the people at the garden – she must have given notice. And you must have known, Richard, didn't you?"

"No I didn't, I swear."

"And who else?" Joel had gone on. "God knows, the mailman, she probably filled out a change of address form. You were all in on this together; you all just let me carry on, jaunty, laughing, skipping in the basement for exercise, arranging my socks just so in my bureau drawer, but most of all, seeming to be a witless asshole."

Richard had been unable to convince Joel that he had not been privy to Gayle's plans. The conversation had ended unpleasantly, and they had not spoken since that day.

Joel let himself in and sat down at the table with Richard. "Shit," he said. "I don't believe this. I guess I should have been paying more attention to the inflection of her voice," he said. "Her voice was so controlled on the telephone and that should have been a sign to me a long time ago, now that I think of it. That's the voice she's been using with me in the last little while, the same voice she used if she had to call the paper boy and ask why the paper was late again."

"Now, if that David guy from Vancouver had happened to call, suddenly there would have been all kinds of inflection, rising voice, falling voice, voice of concern, voice of do you like me and so on and so on. I never really thought about him either until one day about a month ago. I was lying on the couch reading a research article, and I actually remember what the topic was; it was on the validity of hysterical symptoms. All of a sudden I noticed that my palms were sweating and that I had been reading the same line over and over again. The reason for this reaction was that Gayle was laughing, uproariously, about something to do with canna lillies, and talking as if she were on stage somewhere, auditioning. I'd like to know what went on at that bonsai convention. I wonder if that David's there with her now. She didn't mention him on the phone, but anything's possible."

"I don't think that's very likely," Richard said, knowing for certain that David was not with Gayle.

"Well, what is likely?" Joel asked. "When I asked her what all this means she said, 'It doesn't mean anything. I wanted to get away and see some new plant life.' Does that seem very likely? And so I asked, 'But why keep it a secret from me?'"

"And what did she say?" Richard asked, but the question was unnecessary, because Joel was not one to edit conversations he was recounting. It was always a series of I saids, then she saids, then I saids.

"She said," Joel went on, "'I didn't want to say good-bye, you know, face the little send-off rituals and bon voyages, and I knew I'd be returning soon, so I didn't feel a need to say good-bye.' To which I responded with, 'Oh yes you did.'"

Richard knew that he should have expected a bit of a tirade, he knew to expect a kind of Joelish monologue. He fiddled with the newspaper while Joel rattled on.

"Anyway, ultimately she said that it had to do with Elizabeth. 'Elizabeth has such a good memory,' she said, 'It's so mathematical.

There are things I want to discuss with her. She lived with us, you know, when she was sixteen and her mom was sick. And then, afterwards, she was always over at our place. She liked being at our house.'"

"I know," I said, "I know all that. Get to the point."

"Then as a ploy, as a means of appealing to my ego, she began quoting me. 'Remember that time,' she said, 'when you talked about possibilities hitherto not considered, that glance around a corner that returns later in the evening with a sudden yanking wakefulness? Remember when you said that?' she asked."

"I told her that I had been quoting someone else."

"'That doesn't matter,' she said. 'What I have is a case of the sudden yanking wakefulness.'" Joel stopped for a moment, then repeated, "The sudden yanking wakefulness," as if it were the name of a rare tropical disease.

Richard made no comment.

"Richard," Joel said, "did you hear what I just told you? Your sister says she has a case of the sudden yanking wakefulness. Is this an explanation, I want to know? Does it make any particular sense to you?"

Richard's fingertips were becoming grey with printer's ink. He pressed them to his nose, leaving two black smudges, and answered, "No, but if it's any reassurance, I really don't think that David guy is there. I know Gayle well enough that I can almost positively say that."

This seemed to calm Joel and they talked then, for a while, and soon Richard, much to his relief, was watching Joel ease out into traffic, after many nervous shoulder checks.

Richard's stomach was upset. He chewed some minty antacids, realizing that this twinship had often caused him to feel guilty, like an accomplice, with a tormenting set of allegiances. He felt as if he had an entire apartment full of information about Gayle that Joel did not possess, that if he opened a cupboard or closet door, comments, statements and observations would tumble out from times which had been hidden from view.

This David, for example; Richard had met David. The weekend after the conference in Vancouver, Gayle had arranged to meet David at Richard's apartment. Richard had told himself at the time that he did not know or care to know what might go on. He had gone out and left them alone, together, gone to Sandra's house and spent the night and when he returned, they were both gone. The apartment had been left very neat, with the dishes done, the bed made and all of the moulding leftovers tossed out of the fridge and into the garbage. No mention had ever been made.

Richard had taken a picture, though. He liked to do that. It unnerved Gayle, but he could not stop himself from documenting life's brief, disconnected moments. And now an actual likeness of Gayle and David existed, stored in Richard's shoe box of photos.

Richard took the box from his closet shelf and looked carefully at the picture. There he was. David. He had a black beard and wore a turtleneck beneath his shirt and seemed a little out of date. Still, he had some importance. He might somehow have stopped Gayle, restructuring her taxonomy of desires so that a different action might have been taken. He was there on the coast; he could have stopped Gayle at the Lion's Gate Bridge, or buried her feet in the sand and said, "Stay," that most difficult of all commands to obey. Reba, now eight, still did not understand it. On the walks they used to take after work, when Richard and Gayle emerged from the grocery store or the convenience store, Reba would invariably be gone, forcing Gayle to call and call, until the dog came bounding forth from some mysterious mission in the alley.

GAYLE

It is that undecided time of day, late afternoon. Like the little mountain towns in Alberta, the streets are in a kind of rush-hour downtown shade, while above the buildings, there is white life against a blue sky – seagulls and jet trails. The surrounding hills here are so much rounder and more washed away than the Rockies, though, as if this island were only above sea level during the day and slipped below water at night. Perhaps that would explain why there is already mould growing on my sandals.

This morning there was a letter from Richard. When we spoke on the phone, he promised to write every Sunday and so far he has kept to that. I steam the stamps off the envelope and stick them on my bedroom wall; this is how I have decided to mark the passage of time while I am here. Already there are two. Then Elizabeth and I drank mango juice and ate coconut buns from the baker down the street. Afterward there was drip coffee from the Tai Fat Cafe, with evaporated milk, which for me always evokes a holiday mood, and I pondered in a seismic way, "Is it Easter? Christmas?" No, but cause for optimism, though I had that uneasy feeling I get when I realize I most often find happiness in untried places.

It is humid today. Everything is still very new to me here, all of the little details capture my attention. There is a bus, which yesterday took me to a town called Pui O, past an enormous (the world's largest, I have been told) statue of the Buddha. In the village I ate some grassy-flavoured soup in an unlit restaurant with sweating walls, walked for a while, then journeyed home, past the Buddha again who smiled reassuringly as the bus roared by. I delight in the deception that this is how life can proceed, until my money runs out, but I know well enough that this business of novelty is only a petrie dish, as Joel would say, for fiction.

Yesterday I looked through Elizabeth's photo albums; she has all of them here with her, it seems. Maybe it is a characteristic of historians, this hoarding of records and transporting them from continent to continent. There is an album devoted entirely to portraits of Unity, Ontario: Constance Radke selecting her tomato seedlings, John Hammer on his rider lawn mower and so on. There is an album from the time she stayed with us and there are several from afterward. I found the picture of Aunt Peg stepping out of the car when she returned home from the hospital, no longer reddish and plump but hollowed out and the colour of a paper bag. And the picture I took of Elizabeth up in my bedroom, the bedroom we shared, packing her bags to go back home and tend to her mother, and her father. There were pictures of Uncle Ken and his collections of planes and drills and obscure tools, and his shelves of model trucks. You would think he would have had enough of trucks, from driving those Freightliners and Kenworths. And, of course, there were plenty of us, Richard and me and Mom and Dad.

Why did we never take pictures at our house? Why did that Kodak in the brown leather case never move from the bookshelf? It came to be perceived as a paper weight or an ornament, not much different from the cloissoné vase it sat beside.

Not all of Elizabeth's photos are in her albums. There are others I know of stored away in her desk, lying in envelopes, straight and uncomplicated, just as I imagine Elizabeth stores information in her mind. It's as if there were many, many, very thin drawers piled carefully and so compactly in her skull that even during sudden movements, in laughter or surprise, nothing is disturbed. Little coloured rectangles of history; that is what she keeps in her desk drawer and that is what she stacks away in her brain as she reads her dry little texts and her *Journal of History Review*. It will be necessary to search a little more to find the other photos. I would like to see them before I sit down and talk with Elizabeth about Dad.

I am beginning to wonder if perhaps Elizabeth has been teaching for too many years. She has a real zest for herding Jocelyn, Willy, Miranda and me around as if we were junior high students. I have also observed that she loves to pay the bills, or perhaps it is that she loves to know that the bills have been paid; it helps her to feel in control of this mongrel household. Now that I am here, she tells me, the events of each day are held more solidly together. Before, there was always the chance of a cheque being returned NSF. The children were too often left unattended and had been found tampering with the tape recorder. Now the edges are all tucked in, Elizabeth says.

I have seen her walking through the apartment, taking stock of what we need and then heading out to the market. "Batteries and a flashlight," she wrote on a piece of paper yesterday. Elizabeth's idea of a surprise is nearly always something that might guard against catastrophe. She will buy the flashlight and announce that it will be kept in a corner of the cupboard, in case of power failure. She will say that the children may play with it for the following two evenings, and the amazing thing is, they will comply.

Of all of us, Miranda is the most resistant to control, the most unherdable. I do not think that Elizabeth will be happy when she learns that Miranda has lost her job as a half-time secretary. She has been late too many mornings and she has left work early on a few occasions, with no explanation. I can hear Elizabeth commenting on this already. "She's been leaving work early and she only works half-days?" she will ask with over-stated disbelief. Her eyes will bug out of her head and her half-corrected lateral lisp will become apparent, especially if she says, "Jesus Christ," which she will.

Oh well. Tonight I will sit with Miranda and look through the classified section of the *South China Morning Post* for secretarial work. She will be wearing her hat, the hat I have mentioned with the black veil hanging from the brim. It is what the Hakka ladies wear as they haul gravel to construction sites further inland. The people of the village mock Miranda for wearing clothing which is so culturally theirs, but I like to look at her in this hat, I like to look at the face beyond the veil. It is a clever face and a face that speaks its mind and knows its own heart; it is face that seems to be guarding a distant curio and it is fitting that it is so often beneath that wide brim and behind that black veil. Sometimes when I talk to her, I feel as if I am standing at the end of a passageway and peering in at someone I have never met. Except that there is her familiar smile, which is somewhat beautiful, I think. I am waiting for her now to come home, in the way that a person waits for the weather to change or for the rain to come, without really concentrating.

This morning I met Elizabeth's friend, Charlie Reid. He passed beneath our balcony, full-bearded and in paisley print pyjamas. There was some rapid banter in Mandarin, followed by laughter, causing Elizabeth to spill her coffee and splay her legs to allow the drops to fall between. Still, some landed on that barely pigmented skin and I watched it trickle down her calves as she and Charlie shared their absurd little dialogue. I asked myself, do others expect insight and precognition from the red-headed or is it only me? For as long as I can remember, I have selected them as possible bearers of arcane tidings. That woman I saw, for example, on Highway Two, running back to her pickup truck, wearing yellow stockings—an obvious portent, I thought. Her coat was billowing out, a galleon behind her, and I stopped my car to watch her in my rearview mirror because I expected something from her, I don't know what, a word or two that might make all the difference. But, of course, we never met. I sped northward to a talk on "Weed Nomenclature" and she drove on to her, I imagine, more lyrical destination.

I have caught up with Elizabeth now and am almost embarrassed at my destination. There are times I look at her as if she were the yellow-stockinged woman, someone watched and pursued privately, like a movie star or a politician. And when our eyes meet, I have too much gulping action in my throat and I become aware of a pulse in my head as if I possess the baby's soft spot, where there is no bone to hide the lively throbbing of the blood. She is not, after all, Meryl Streep or Pierre Trudeau. Why must I be so nervous? It was all so long ago.

"Can you dance?" Elizabeth asked Charlie.

"No, I can't dance. Can you dance?" Charlie answered.

"No, but I wish very much to learn."

This dialogue was conducted in English, for my benefit. It was an example of what Elizabeth has learned through self-instruction with tapes and a book titled *Teach Yourself Mandarin*. She wanted me to know why she laughs, why there are the solitary "har hars" as she sits in her bedroom listening to her language tapes.

"Come for lunch," Charlie said, and soon we were walking the board and concrete pathways through the rice seedlings to his house. I like to study the rice which changes colour daily, yearning, it seems, for a depth of green that is always one day beyond. Charlie's house is in the interior, further than the rice, beyond trails bordered by fig and banana trees and children in shorts and plastic shoes. A woman with a face shaped like an elm leaf, Pui Sin, lives with Charlie. She has one eye whited over with a cataract. Pui Sin held up one hand when we arrived, as if to arrest the sound of Elizabeth's bleating Mandarin, then shook her head and brought us inside.

We sat at the table drinking tea. There were fish, which Pui Sin gutted, her tea cup quickly becoming glued with scales, and other things, too many things, the place is cluttered actually, and there is much to look at. On Charlie's fridge there is a poster with a quote from an American senator who in 1940 said, "With God's help we will lift Shanghai up, ever up, until it is just like Kansas City." Charlie lived in Shanghai for years, working with Shell Oil until 1957, when the British employees were asked to leave. He knew Edward Snow and he uses old-fashioned words such as vainglorious.

I examined Charlie's bookshelves while the others talked, and discovered a volume called *Figs of Hong Kong*. I had forgotten about the wasps and figs and their symbiotic relationship. Wasps pollinate figs and figs create a damp and sugary uterus within which wasps develop and reproduce. Such a robust little circle of life.

Charlie insisted that I borrow the book. "It's unbecoming that I own such a thing," he said. "The only book I possess that deals with plants or agriculture. There was a book-burning you know, one of the biggest ever, back in the days of Emperor Chin Shih Huang-ti. He and his men concluded that books dealing with divination, medicine and farming were all that was necessary to run an empire. The rest were torched. If you tried to conceal any literature, you soon found yourself carting rocks to the Great Wall. Think of all that was lost! So, it's just my way of commemorating those folks, keeping divination and so on off my shelves, and I include religion in that broad category. I don't know how I came to own the fig book, but let's just call it a farming text and I'll vouchsafe it to you."

Charlie stood and walked to his ancient, round-shouldered fridge where he withdrew a bottle of white, glistening liquid. After taking a swig he said, "Fish oil. I drink it as a chaser to everything."

Lunch was a slow process and eventually Miranda's children arrived on their way home from school. Pui Sin dotes on them, feeding them egg tarts and allowing unlimited plundering of the garden. Charlie asked Jocelyn about her mother and I listened carefully to her reply but could not understand.

They are such peculiar children, especially Jocelyn with her suspiciously set mouth and her accent. Cantonese is their first language, now that they have been here for so long. If her speech could be set in colour, it would be all pastels; in shape, no angles. She asked Charlie for "seesos," meaning scissors, then a brush, so as to play hairdresser with me, then silently snipped around my head, and brushed my hair while we sat in the garden.

The four of us walked back home together and Elizabeth left immediately for work. The kids are out now, maybe in the market or on the beach. Miranda did not arrive on the four o'clock ferry, which means she may be here at half-past four or five or six o'clock or who knows when – she is looking for work – and that I may have to cook for Jocelyn and Willy. This irresponsibility irks Elizabeth, but, I must admit, I am not so critical. The children are easy companions and Miranda can disarm me with nothing more than her voice and the rate at which she talks and the offhand manner in which she discloses the sort of information that I would keep secret for years. It dispels some of the circumspection I have brought here with me.

For now, what I will do is sit on the balcony and watch the

people walking below. They dress in silk and cotton and straw and I imagine them to be comfortable, in the same dimming light their ancestors knew. Inside, though, for everyone, there must always be a bead of perspiration, just a bit of the trembling palsy. I can't be the only one.

Richard

Richard was considering buying a car. It would get me out of the house, he thought. Why a grown man like me does not own a car, I do not know, Richard said to himself and then shuddered, as if at a striking bit of evidence brought forth at a trial. "We could go for drives," he said to Reba, who had been dropped off by Joel a few days earlier. Richard knew, before he had completed this thought, that any new goals, any new plans were out of the question until he could begin to feel at least a bit more at ease in his own home. He was going to stick with this goal, yes he was. Besides, he did not have the money for a car and he hated the idea of borrowing.

It had been one of his motives for moving from Ontario to Alberta, this ever far-off plan to buy a car. He and Gayle had moved west together in 1981, following Elizabeth who had transplanted herself in 1979. All three had enjoyed a playful period of steady employment and charge cards and Bloody Marys and flights to Hawaii; the Arkadian Epoch, they had dubbed it later on. After several years though, only Elizabeth had accumulated retirement savings plans, new Toyotas and so on. Richard and Gayle had been profligate. And Joel was not much different.

Gayle had met Joel while he was still a graduate student, working as a teaching assistant, finishing his thesis, energetically hating it all, and she was working for the university grounds department. For two years, Gayle, Richard and Joel had been together at the same institution, which had prompted Richard to observe once that the situation was like being triplets, having the same mother, being in the care of the one big cheque-printer. It had always seemed a little alien to them that Elizabeth received paycheques from the school board which were green and white, and it became a joke that, because she was more prudent with money, Elizabeth's cheques were in some way more durable than the university's blue and white ones.

Working together, Richard, Gayle and Joel had nearly always met for lunch in the crowded dining rooms. Richard became a bit sentimental as he recalled circumstances which had presented themselves to them: a fine art student with woodcuts to illustrate "A Child's Christmas in Wales," or the group of philosophy students with poor posture and frail stature they had labelled "The Rickets Five."

Often they had taken walks to the greenhouse, in particular the tropical house, which was Gayle's favourite. Richard had always felt somewhat nervous there, as if those stamens and anthers might pollinate anything, might harpoon their furriness on to human skin and, days later, cause lumps to form and plots of succulents to burst forth. Richard had to admit that he had never been too confident in the genetic discreteness of species; what was there, really, to prevent a bit of biological tomfoolery from occurring?

"I prefer these nice, cool hallways," Richard said once to Gayle, as they left the greenhouses and entered a work area filled with peat pots and wheelbarrows and latched doors leading to walk-in refrigerators filled with cold, hardy bits of life that knew, (Gayle liked to point out in support of plants) exactly how to measure the lengthening of the days.

Those years had been a festive time, the way work can be in the best of circumstances. But Joel had finished his degree and gone to work with Mental Health, and Gayle had moved to the city gardens so that now only Richard remained at the library. There was Sandra, of course, but that was different, because there were noon hours when he avoided her.

Sandra was a woman Richard saw. That is how he described it to himself and others. "Sandra is a woman I am seeing," he would say to the peple who asked, and there were several, because Richard and Sandra were rarely seen together. What they did publicly was play bridge; their private activities included sleeping together occasionally.

Sandra wore quantities of jewellery, gold rings on one hand and silver on the other. She had allergies and was prone to worrying about her humidifiers and air conditioners and the dust in Calgary. She rarely visited Richard's apartment because of its proximity to Memorial Drive and the fumes, and her discomfort away from her own, controlled environment. It seemed to Richard that Sandra's concerns about devices related to air quality had generalized to all appliances, big or small, electrical or mechanical; she was absolutely intolerant of breakage. Once, a malfunction in the snooze function of her clock radio had caused Sandra to confess to Richard that when anything electrical did not work properly, she longed to plug it in and drop it into a tub of water so that it could electrocute itself and all of its unreliable wires could be melted into one huge, smoking knot of revenge. When Richard thought about Sandra, this image often sprang to mind.

Richard and Sandra had known one another for eighteen months and normally talked on the telephone every other day. Since Gayle had left, twenty days ago, Richard had only called twice and often did not answer the phone when he thought it might be Sandra calling. He did not know why; it was all part of this uneasiness that had set in, it was all part of this discomfort in his own home, and it was all part of a strengthening need to scan newspapers and, at work, journals, for references to the small and the inexplicable.

Yes, it seemed that as Sandra faded in significance, the Brieflies were becoming more and more compelling to Richard. He likened them to pulsars, stars that have shrunk to the size of a small city.

Each word had more weight, less volume and a greater specific density. He imagined if he clipped a single phrase and dropped it to the floor, it might smash through the apartment beneath him to the waterworks and boilers below.

Tonight he read, "Soviet Filmmakers Die in Freak Blizzard" and he was caught with the sensation of having lost all of his milestones and landmarks and companions. He was made temporarily dizzy by the thought of a wild and sudden snowfall in Siberia and the panic of the filmmakers. Still, he could find plenty of reassurance evinced from all that he knew about the Soviet Union: the race to meet production quotas, control panels glued on to appliances with wires left dangling and unconnected inside televisions, radios and possibly snowmobiles. Faulty snowmobiles must have been the cause, Richard thought. The factory's quota to the state trading board had not been met; things were rushed. A search party had been sent out on poorly constructed snowmobiles which had broken down. Tapestries of information and coincidence shaped themselves into a reason, and for a moment, Richard was content.

He poured some tea. It was another Wednesday after work. Richard always rushed home for just this: to climb two creaking sets of stairs to his apartment, which was the attic floor of an old yellow brick house, and sit with a pot of tea, Monday through Thursday, or a vodka martini on Fridays. Times and schedules were his only fastidiousness. It was as if he believed that, without scheduling his after-work behaviour – drinking, eating, recreation, enrichment, good works – he would go completely off the rails and in a matter of days would become a vagrant, an alcoholic, someone with no plans, someone who thinks only of himself.

Knowing that an unscheduled evening lay ahead, Richard drank his tea on this June evening, therefore, with some apprehension. He missed the habit of eating out with Gayle and Joel on Wednesdays. So much of his life had been a coupling with Gayle that, for a moment, Richard feared that the loss of the carburetion process, the combustion brought about by their relationship, would cause him to become so ennervated that he would have to lie down for a long time, take to his bed in the way dissatisfied women of his grandparents' generation had been known to do. But Richard knew that he was much too tall and thin for such drama to be appropriate.

Instead, he had a sudden memory of his father talking to them one day as they piled wood. "Doppelgangers," he had said, as he so often did when he wanted to address Richard and Gayle collectively, "it's the most critical job to fix your gaze on the backside of change." They had been stacking for a while, were maybe half-finished. "Just look there at the woodpile," he had said, "and then at the wood still on the ground to get a certain knowledge of all of the details of possibility, of the hundreds of ways the jigsaw puzzle might have been formed. There really are no loops and tabs for joining parts together. There really is no way in which events must unfold. Everything can be undone. Or done in a different way. People tend to forget that."

That day, they had only worried that Duncan would insist that the wood be unpiled and stacked in another way. Now, Richard thought, maybe his father had had a point; quite often he did, after all. I could go out for dinner with Joel, he thought, there is no reason why I couldn't do that. I should call him.

But Richard became distracted then, by memories of his father. Duncan had been OK that summer they had piled the wood together, a little high maybe, but no indication that a few months later he would be off again, leaving those notes and sitting in the living room listening to the same records over and over again.

Richard had the notes that Duncan had left during his final year. They were in a black film canister which Gayle had left with Richard years ago saying she didn't have the heart to destroy them but she also did not have the heart to keep them. All had been addressed to Gayle and found beneath the fossil on her dresser first thing in the morning. Gayle had told Richard once that the first note had given her the strangest sensation, of a daughter having been planted in the place where a mother might have been. She said that, with the first note, she felt as if she could not walk properly, as if their mother's brown tweed suit, intended for her tallness and girth, were hanging without sufficient flesh on Gayle's shoulders.

There had been four notes altogether (only three remained) and Richard decided that he should take a look at them one more time. He found the little container on his bookshelf, sat down and poured out the bits of paper. They were small and almost illegible, having been folded time and again by nervous hands so that the pencil markings were a rubbed and vanishing grey. Richard read aloud and with great solemnity to Reba. "'Paper covers rock,' 'Your father regrets,'" and "'Your mother does not hear.' I can actually almost laugh at these nonsensical snippets now, Reba," he added.

Years ago, though, he and Gayle had puzzled over these notes, especially the first. "Your mother does not hear." Although they were then eleven, and of an age to suspect that it referred to something other than acuity of hearing, both could not help conducting tests. They had dropped pencils, or paper clips, behind Louise's back, or whispered as she read. "What the hell is up with you two?" she would eventually ask, while lighting a cigarette. Louise kept a box of wooden matches with her du Mauriers, which were never far from hand. She smoked while listening to the radio and watching TV, talking on the telephone and reading. Cigarettes seemed to be an accessory to communication for her, and Richard and Gayle finally took this to indicate that her hearing was better than average. Partial deafness would have forced her to pay more attention, listen up with a straight back and certainly not be lighting and puffing and saying, "Hand me that ashtray there, will you Gayle?"

Then, wondering if the note referred to some inattentiveness in their mother, Richard and Gayle had managed to get a tape recording of a conversation between their parents. The little tape recorder had been left on, working silently on the bookcase, capturing Duncan's silence, the late news, the turning pages of Louise's magazine and the sounds of fingers rummaging through a bowl of nuts left over from Thanksgiving.

Louise had begun the conversation by saying, "Some of the Amish were over today to see Gayle and Richard. That Mary, the oldest one, I was looking at her and you know, she is built just like a boy, no hips to speak of and arms like a weight-lifter. They must work her. I wonder that some of those kids don't run away."

And Duncan had replied, "Well, I guess that Raymond Baetz has stayed put since they brought him back from Kitchener. They burned the clothes he bought but other than that, I don't think much came of it. Maybe he decided he liked that way of life after all. In some ways it might be a relief, to have no decisions to make."

There had been an almost imperceptible puff, an exhalation of mild disapproval from Louise's nostrils, followed by more rattling of nuts and breaking of shells. Then the television was turned off, the scraping of chair legs on linoleum was heard, light switches were flipped, and the tape continued to spin until Gayle crept downstairs to retrieve it.

Richard and Gayle must have listened to the Amish conversation at least twenty times over the course of that fall, not so much because of its content, but because there were times by then, only a few, when both would have admitted to being a little afraid of their father. Must have been the clattering of the nuts that comforted us, Richard thought. Maybe it caused us to feel that secure preparedness we all long to feel in autumn, that pioneer sensation of root cellars and granaries filled. Or maybe we sensed that he was on his way out, after that swimming incident, although Gayle would certainly never own up to that.

It had happened on the last Sunday of September, and they had picked elderberries, as usual. The last Sunday of September was set aside for elderberries, which were frozen and made into pies throughout the winter, elderberries with their smokiness and yeastiness, never really good to taste, Richard realized, as if decay must set in with maturity.

After the berries had been picked, Duncan insisted on walking to the lake for his final swim of the year, and instead of taking the road, they had taken the steep trail, the cat-walk it was called, at the back of their farm, to the water's edge. This had marked the swim as an event because the cat-walk was off limits from Labour Day until Victoria Day. When Richard and Gayle were very young a neighbour boy had taken that pathway to the lake one March afternoon, slipped on the frozen earth and broken his back. Thereafter, for the McDonagh children, the cat-walk season was strictly imposed.

That Sunday, though, the Sunday of the final swim, the catwalk had been a disappointment – they were old enough by then that the breaking of convention had begun to lose its attraction. The beach was desolate, devoid of its holiday soul. There had been a feeling of being at the fairgrounds after the midway had been packed up. Louise had forgotten to bring along the soda pop, and the blanket she usually sat upon was wrapped around her shoulders. She sat digging in the sand with her right hand, looking out at the water, which was unusual for her; Louise rarely rested like that. Only when she was gathering the eggs or hoeing the garden did she allow her face to loosen with thoughtlessness. Richard remembered rambling in the sand and Gayle wading to her knees while Duncan plunged in, claiming that he would swim halfway to Bay City, Michigan. He had made this type of boast before. Often, he would dive down as far as possible, a great distance from the shore, and return with tales of lost freighters or forests of underwater trees, aquabors, he called them. This type of behaviour had become an embarrassment to Richard by then.

Duncan swam out further than ever that day, an uneasy distance, so that Louise, after a few minutes, said to Gayle, "Come here, we'll spread out the blanket and you can sit with me."

For a while he disappeared altogether, diving downward they had guessed, gone like the loon, and Louise's face firmed up again, the way it would when she had phone calls to make or letters to write. She dug into the coarse, wet sand, marbled with white and yellowish stones. Gayle pressed a hand to her breast bone. Richard stood, thinking, "Must be behind a wave." But the lake was calm that day, calmer than the Sunday CBC radio voices from Louise's little transistor.

"There he is," Gayle said at last and Louise turned off the radio and they all stood and watched as he swam back to them, throwing silver dollars into the sunlight. At the water's edge, Gayle had grabbed at Duncan's arms while Louise bent down to plunge her hand into the water, sand detaching itself with the same ease she seemed to behold her marriage.

"What happened?" Gayle cried. "You were under water for one hundred and thirty-five beats of my heart." But there was no answer from Duncan. He had a look on his face that Richard remembered though, from where he had stayed on the sand watching. It was an expression that became more and more familiar that year, a departing look, the absent-minded gaze of someone going elsewhere.

"Gayle looked that way too, before she left. I just realized that now," Richard said to the dog, pondering his new tendency to speak out loud while alone, his sudden lack of companionship, and his laziness, the many facets of his laziness. He did not contact others enough, he did not call Sandra and he rode around in his chair too much of the time.

Richard owned a wheeled stenographer's chair which he had bought at an auction of used office furniture. Much of his life was conducted from this chair which rolled easily from the table to the refrigerator. The idea had come from Richard's ophthalmologist who wheeled about his office, actually lifting his feet from the floor to scoot from one type of vision apparatus to another. Even though this eye doctor was obese, Richard admired him for his smooth carriage. And, during a moment of appreciation for his ophthalmologist, Richard rode to his telephone at last, to call Joel and arrange dinner out with him. Then he felt as if a degree of order had been maintained.

Half an hour later, Joel was there, looking dishevelled in a grey sweatshirt and shorts, very white legs and very white feet which appeared grey also, where they met his sandals. He had been out the night before, to a Mental Health dance with some of his clients, the aimless, the wanderers, and the instant coffee drinkers living in rooming houses and in government supervised basements.

"This was so weird. I danced with a woman last night," Joel said, starting to talk before they had even edged their way into traffic, "who swore she knew me, but I know I've never seen her before. We had only been dancing for seconds, it was a two-step and I was having a hard time keeping up with her, when she said to me, with the emphasis on *you're*, 'You're one,' you know, with heavy significance, and I of course asked, 'Of what?,' even though I should have known better."

Joel attempted to adjust his outside mirror while he talked. "So, in answer to my question she said, 'One of the empaths.' And I said, trying for a more upbeat mood, 'That's a "Star Trek" word, isn't it?'"

"She ignored this comment and said, 'Yes, one who takes the pain.' And the way she was looking at me and her voice," Joel said, "her voice I cannot describe, but anyway, it almost finished me off because I realized all of a sudden that she might be able to hand something over to me right then and there, in the Scandinavian Club Hall, some pain, maybe not in a package or an envelope but through some kind of exchange, electrical or metaphysical."

Richard noticed that Joel's hair was flattened against his head at the back, as if he had just gotten out of bed.

"Anyway," Joel went on, "I had a sudden fear that there would be a type of I don't know – maybe strobe action between us on the dance floor, maybe the smell of singed hair? I don't know – I just had to get out of there, it was more unusually weird than it usually is and people kept asking about Gayle. But the really weird thing is, I feel different today. I think I did take her pain. She's probably down at the Bay right now trying on dresses and buying make-up. She's probably phoned for a few job interviews. While I now feel, for certain, that Gayle is gone for good. How long will I have to carry this around?" Joel asked, half playfully, half fearfully. "How long 'til I find another empath to heave it to?"

"Oh, she'll be back," Richard said, looking through the tape case and wondering as he always did about Joel's taste in music. "All this bluegrass stuff is so wholesome," he commented. "What did you tell them when they asked about Gayle? Who asked, anyway, the crazies you work with or the ones you try to help?"

"Both sets," Joel answered. "And I gave different answers to everyone, which is what I think paved the way for me to receive the pain. I was like an empath-in-waiting, I guess. I told Robin – the man who keeps hanging around City Hall waiting for an appointment, I've told you about him, haven't I? – that Gayle had gone on a holiday, and he said, 'Separate vacations are a sign of strength in a marriage, I think.' His voice is really high and irritating and all of a sudden everything that I don't like about my job washed over me and I wanted to get rid of him, so made the mistake of sitting with Julia and Steve for a while. They asked too, of course, but they had already heard things, so I had to attempt a truthful response. 'She's in Hong Kong to see a cousin. Wanted some time to herself,' I said. They were concerned but wanted details, you know these mental health types. So I disengaged myself from them and that's when the dance occurred and I left soon after, sparks flying from my ass probably, like a friction toy."

Richard gave up on finding any music he would want to hear, snapped the case shut and flinging it into the back seat said, "You don't have to explain Gayle's behaviour, or your behaviour, to Julia and Steve. I've met them, I know what they're like. They're morbid, they like pain, they only watch the late news when there's been a disaster. I know, because I'm like that too. So, avoid them is my advice." And then Richard added, gesturing to the television set which had been in the back seat for weeks, "You still haven't had that thing fixed."

"I know. I'm growing to like its company in the car. I may move it to the front seat. You know that song about only being lonely when I'm driving in my car. It's kind of true for me. So now, I just look in my rearview mirror and see that TV screen back there. Good company, nice face, a bit Herman Munsterish but still, as my mother says, better than nothing."

Joel turned the windshield wipers on and off repeatedly, spraying the windshield with washer fluid. He was crankier suddenly, it seemed to Richard, perhaps because he had partially admitted to his loneliness and perhaps because the windshield was smeared with insects.

"This damned car is no good. Not even an intermittent option for the wipers." Then, without even a pause, Joel said, "I hate to say this to you, her brother, but the way I feel right now, right this moment, I would like to, I don't know, choke Gayle maybe, or punch her. Yes, I think a right jab to the shoulder muscle, hard enough to achieve that muscle ache, is what I'm thinking of. I know I'm not supposed to think that sort of thing. I know what Julia would say if she heard me talking like this. She'd say, 'to defuse aggression,'" and at this point Joel began mimicking Julia's tendency to overly sibilate her s's, "'in the midst of an argument, you must stop shouting and begin whispering, change tracks without any warning.'" Joel became himself again and said, "That's what she and Steve do. This whispering fixes everything up. Maybe if I phoned Gayle and whispered across the Pacific, 'You fucking bitch,' everything would be all right."

Richard said, "There's a stop here," and the car came to a halt in the middle of an intersection. They backed up. People stared from the sidewalk and a boy on a skateboard flicked his hair back and laughed.

Richard wanted to be understanding, because he knew Gayle's leaving had been unkind, because Joel's car was such a wreck, and because he disliked Julia and Steve, but it was not possible. Cautiously, he said, "Well, there are times when I think she was really wrong to leave like that and then I think, and I know this is really conventional logic, but I think it anyway, that you two weren't married, so she was free to do what she wanted. I know that makes no sense, but . . . "

"But, she's your sister, and brothers have this thing about their sisters, right?" Joel interrupted, "that they should be little replicas of their mothers. Well, I want you to know that proposals had been made, by me, and who knows, probably by two or three others, not to mention those plant assholes from B.C. she kept bringing home and reconnoitering with. Even that Jackie woman may have proposed. I don't know – I'm sure you know more than I do."

Joel stopped the car and began rummaging in the glove box for an ice scraper which he used to attempt to remove some of the bugs from the windshield. The sun had come out and now their entrails created rainbow-hued arcs on the glass. Getting back inside he said, "Gayle is the most unmarrying person I know; she might even be the most unloving, for that matter. I mean, when it comes to the boring, enduring kind of love. As soon as it becomes a little too aesthetically familiar, she's gone. You know, she's arranged the flowers in as many ways as she possibly can, she has bought me all the shirts she wants to dress me in, the furniture has been moved around and she has taken my picture with all of the different coloured lenses she owns – as soon as that's all done, it's over. It'll be the same for the next person. That's my only consolation."

Richard was relieved when they arrived at the restaurant, Joel's favourite, the Queen's Plate, where there were always steamy windows and snake plants and two waitresses sitting at the back table with word finds and crosswords. Richard was also gladdened to see the afternoon edition of the national paper, as it was called, still in the stands. Something to buy and read aloud to Joel. Although Richard had been asked in many situations to stop reading aloud, he still looked forward to it as a person will anticipate listening to a certain song or watching a boxing match, knowing that steady, undeniable pleasure will be had.

But inside, seated, Joel continued to talk, foiling Richard's plan to begin a presentation of the lesser current events.

"The one thing that Gayle and I have in common," Joel said, "is that neither of us can let an idea die, you know, just pass away. Once there is a plan in mind, we have to pursue it like a rolling stone downhill. And if this stone happens to come to rest from inertia or travels into a ditch where it belongs, we will nudge the thing back onto the pathway until it hits bottom and absolutely ceases to rock back and forth." Joel took a deep breath and said, "At which point, if we're talking about Gayle, it would be kicked into one last gasp of motion. It just seems that, most times, my intentions have been more benign than hers and would involve, say, several evenings at the Regent Hotel watching the clientele until I got bored, or four or five phone calls in the night until I had located Janie Linder, just to find out what she's thinking about these times. Not Gayle though. No. Global plans for that one, excursion fare tickets to far-off places with no satisfaction in sight."

Joel's face had become red and, unsure how to respond with those hands occasionally slapping down upon his newspaper as they were, Richard asked, "Do you mind if we change the subject?"

"No, I don't mind, actually," Joel responded, calming down suddenly. "I'd like to change the subject. Why don't we? I'd like to change it to food. Let's look at the menu."

As they studied the menu, Richard began listening to a man sitting at the counter. He was very thin and was saying, "I got thrown out of that place once for unplugging the juke box. You ever notice how there's noise everywhere you go nowadays? You can't escape. I say to people, if you're listening to noise you can be sure of one thing and that is that you're not thinking." The owner, behind the counter, was looking through the snake plants and on to the street.

And at that moment, although there was no noise to speak of, and less activity, Richard felt surrounded by a kind of suppressed and greasy-flavoured chaos which seemed to be with him everywhere lately, not just at the Queen's Plate. This old man at the counter was to be envied, really, he supposed, whatever his older and more threadbare sensibilities might happen to be, his loyalty to certain standards and codes, the code of the foxtrot, the code of draught beer for a quarter or the code of speaking out freely in restaurants with no audience at all. No taking off to Asia for him. Richard had a feeling that this man had led his life in a way that would prevent it ever becoming a brief newspaper account and this was good, he thought. This was very good.

GAYLE

Elizabeth has gone to work and Miranda has taken the children into Hong Kong so that they can spend the day with their father. And I am alone in this apartment for the first time in almost a month. It is early evening here, the noisiest time of the day because the television sets have been turned on. They are all portable, it seems, and their owners place them in doorways, these TV's, and then sit or stand outside in semi-circular formation, watching. Most nights it is as if a festival of street performance were occurring.

But I have been up here in this poorly lit place, in another not-so-festive atmosphere, sitting at Elizabeth's desk, searching for the slides I knew she would have with her here. I am almost positive no one else has ever seen them, not Richard, or Mother. These little images were forgotten in the midst of all the brouhaha.

Throughout my methodical investigation, Elizabeth's reel-to-reel has sat watching me, looking as if I should at least tell it what I am doing, but I have not. So many things have been removed from this desk, one by one, the files, the magazines, the pictures, each one being returned to precisely the same spot, leaving behind no sign of my invasion. What strange artifacts our cousin has chosen to bring around the world with her. There was a collection of *Star Weekly*'s from 1966 and 1967. Were these important years for Elizabeth, I wonder, or does she just like those old advertisements for Sanforization and Sanforization Plus? And there were files on all of us, as I should have expected, Richard, me, Peg, Ken and Mother not to mention Simone de Beauvoir and Pol Pot. Nothing on Dad. I looked through everything pertaining to us or any blood relation. Richard's and mine and Peg's were largely made up of correspondence. Mother's file held the scrapbook of newspaper clippings Elizabeth kept on her, along with several copies of election campaign flyers.

I was nervous, digging through these bones, even with the content being so mundane. My hands trembled and every few minutes I went to the balcony to look for Elizabeth, who still is under the impression I am just here for a visit, or at the street, or at my laundry hanging from a bamboo pole. With each trip the street was a little darker and the television sets burned a little more boldly, all reds and yellows. This brilliant demonstration of the mindless power of electric light seemed to give me the courage I required to return to my excavating. Maybe unbeknownst to us humans, television and all of the other man-made sources of light, have a photosynthetic effect; maybe we possess trace amounts of chlorophyll in our bloodstreams which allows us to make use of the light from our lamps and film projectors. I hope so.

The boxes of slides were at the back of Elizabeth's second desk drawer. By the time I located them, the mah-jong cubes were beginning to stir, whirring like wings down in the street, causing me to hurry a bit and sweat a bit. I considered how ironic it would be to discover that those slides were actually still back in Unity, on a closet shelf perhaps. I thought of the pathetic marksmanship involved in missing a target by half a planet, talking out loud to myself as I dropped entire boxes of slides. In picking them up, my fingers would become oddly weak and limp, as in a very bad dream when a knot must be untied or a key turned to escape imminent death, and the muscles and the mind appear to have lost their connection.

There were twenty-six little yellow boxes. I knew what to look for though; I knew that the pictures of cloud formations Elizabeth had used for her science fair exhibit were in the same container as the slides I wanted. And sure enough, at last I found cirrus. I returned it to its box and walked to the balcony for a breath of air. Eight-thirty it was then and the street was in full throttle, with even the communists from the next door playing their triumphant, scratched and revolutionary records from the rooftop. The world seemed safely preoccupied without me. There was no sign of Elizabeth, so I went back inside and held cirrus to the light once more. Then stratus. Then each of them, very quickly, and packed them away and hid them behind the books in my Pepsi crate.

I began to worry then that in my haste I had somehow disturbed the contents of Elizabeth's desk or altered the papers on its surface. By way of possible explanation for this, I decided to say that I had used the desk to write a letter. And, whenever I tell lies, I find that I must rehearse my story, word for word, no matter how banal. "I've been writing a letter," I said confidently to no one, swivelling in Elizabeth's desk chair. "The light's better here than in the hallway and my Pepsi crate could hardly be considered a desk." This I repeated three times.

It is necessary to be a bit under-handed because Elizabeth has managed, in her quiet and thorough way, to keep these slides from me. If I had asked for them, she would have put me off in some way as she has in the past. "Oh, they're somewhere around. I'll look later." But she never has. The only time I ever saw them was at the science fair.

I wonder if Richard remembers the science fair the first time we went, when Elizabeth had her cloud exhibit. I had never been to the high school before and it seemed such a romantic and scholarly place – Unity Collegiate – I even loved the name. Everything that intellect and reason brought to mind in youth – gas taps, long black-topped desks, rolls and rolls of maps – all housed in that yellow brick building. I was moved by the occasion, even though I was not at all in my right mind, Dad having been gone for only about twelve weeks. I was still wearing those huge, white shirts of his. But Aunt Peg insisted on taking us. She was getting better and stronger every day; she wanted to be back at work, back in the classroom where she belonged.

The gymnasium was filled with serious-minded young people, judges in lab coats, and parents, and I know Richard must recall the looks we got. We were an exhibit in and of ourselves, I suppose, of some principle or other, perhaps more social than scientific, and therefore a little inappropriate and a little exciting. Wherever we walked a protective bubble of distance surrounded us, like a cell wall.

Of all the displays, Elizabeth's is the only one I can bring to mind. She had blown several cloud photographs up to poster size and had a continuous slide show going on weather systems. That was the topic. And it was a very popular one, being so accessible, the judges said later, and relevant to the community. Everyone had wanted to see the black clouds rolling in over the lake and the Formans' sugar bush against a February sky.

A hundred more possible locations to look for Dad came to mind as I watched back then; a hundred possible directions in which he might have gone and a hundred possible reasons for going. And I remember beginning to believe, up on the darkened stage, in Elizabeth's little corner of the science fair, that this problem could be solved. I felt those citizens' large and sensible bodies behind me and beside me like proverbs in a time of despair, ideas that would stop all nonsense, that would not allow for an adult man to be in a hiding place much longer.

Then I heard someone behind me whisper, "That's the McDonagh girl," and I was no longer sure of things. I moved in behind the table and sat with Elizabeth who made no comment about my shirt or the expression on my face.

And that is when I first saw those slides. I knew she had taken pictures that night, but had not thought about them until then. Sitting next to Elizabeth, on one of those noisy stacking chairs with U.C. stamped possessively on the back, I began glancing through the slides Elizabeth had brought along in flat yellow boxes, those she had not included in her exhibit, holding them up to the wire-protected lights above the gymnasium floor. I looked again and again, knowing that while others saw only squares of blackness held above a squinting face, I saw the kitchen, Richard,

Dad and me, the pail with the fish in it, the steaming kettle. All around me was talk, soft murmuring approval of youth and effort while I, I was gone, pulled by the eyes into a place no one else could follow, a two-dimensional place, a cartoonishly bright imitation of past days. I wanted to look and look, without letting on to Elizabeth how much so.

Just as I am tonight.

Elizabeth was on to me, though, and as we dismantled the exhibit she was very careful to take all of the slides and pack them together. She must have kept them hidden in her room, then taken them off to university with her, always out of reach. These images have been guarded like valuable and delicate heirlooms, as if they were rightfully hers, as if through some little known tradition of tribal inheritance, the niece, not the daughter, should possess the last moments of the vanished father.

Gayle

Now we have a new day and another letter from Richard. Three Canadian stamps, three tiny Canadian flags, wave briskly in a row above my Pepsi crate. But there is not a breath of wind on this island, nothing to cause the heavy air to move along. Humidity is here with me, has become my companion, line upon line of wet muslin giving the impression that it would like to fall to the floor. Perhaps it should.

I have that uneasy feeling that I am about to disgrace myself in some way, or should I say, another way. My writing becomes more cramped and the letters smaller. Perhaps I need a code, such as we had in the third grade; put 'a' at the end of the alphabet and move each letter one position to the left. FZXKD was my name. It seemed so space age, so intergalactic, at the time.

I have some questions for the atmospheric pressure. I would

like to ask someone, the judge of all things profane, the ruler of the unhallowed halls, one who is most expert in the phenomenon of backsliding – Do I have no depth? And that is not the only question I would ask, there are others (and I would ask these specialists in irreverence because I am serious about wanting the truth). I would ask, do others form deep and lasting attractions, rapturous in their complexity, discovering each day a newness in their mates which causes an excited longing to rush home from work? I would ask, is there such viscosity to their attachments that the blood slows so that it can transport something more vital than delight?

I do not know. Why are there not government handbooks devoted to such questions, as there are on pruning and grafting?

There is a new problem, a new distraction. Male, female – it does not matter, as long as I am pulled a bit from my path. It is this Miranda who is living here. It seems to take no time at all for these erotic interests to ignite for me. With David and Jackie it was the same. Although I do not believe in any hocus-pocus, I like to imagine in these situations that someone, someone in a clerical position, the secretary of all hankering, has phoned ahead and arranged for it to be so. With Jackie, we were in adjoining rooms, at the perennials conference, with so much running back and forth and tentative morning knocking. Nothing happened though. We managed to keep ourselves most often among a group of gardeners, protected by them and the overhanging branches and the false colours of the hydrangea. People who love plants are tied to the organic, I find, but strangely slackened from the personal. We talk of stamens and anthers and pollination. Pistils. We break apart furry seed pods to examine the interior of fruit and juice, dipping in fingers, licking the tips, tasting bitterness like quinine. Glabrous we say, or succulent. Then we turn back to our work with shrubs and fungus. At least, that is what I did, that time in Vancouver.

Still, we smiled awfully broadly when we met, Jackie and I, so mutually, as if I knew her language as well as she. I had no idea we were using two separate dictionaries. It was not until much later, back home, after her third phone call, that I had an inkling of the sort that causes weeks of missed innuendo to unfurl before the mind, like learning to read must have felt. Jackie said, "I'd love it if you could come out for a weekend," and something in the timbre of this resonated elsewhere. And there it was. The translation began to make sense, despite the fact that it was a bad translation, driven by suspicion.

"Chasmophytes," Jackie said over the phone another time, "I'm going to Kamloops to collect some chasmophytes, you know, rock-loving, crevice-growing plants. Want to meet me there?"

"What does she mean, chasm? She's making fun of me with the use of these words, crevice-growing," I said to myself, deciding to drive out, leave at four in the morning, spend the day and come back.

The cacti in Kamloops were surprising, up on the grey-green hills. Jackie rubbed sage between her fingers, then held them to my nose. We walked and crouched together to examine blossoms and by the time she had mentioned her friend Maura three or four times, I had decided not to stay a moment past dinner. It was a weekend and I could have and part of me wanted to, but instead I talked rapidly and without stop which is a technique I have discovered that discourages questioning. I told her that it was my autonomic nervous system, at least that was Joel's explanation. I used Joel's name several times. I said, "Joel believes that people idle at different rates and don't like to let the cycles per second go slower than the speed that is customary for them. They're afraid of a stall, so they look for fuel. Different people have different fuels, you know, leaded, unleaded, high octane, insecurity, passion, hate. That's the sort of thing Joel likes to think about."

"Maybe that's what's wrong with Maura," Jackie said. "She idles at too fast a rate and that's why she sleeps like a wolf or a dog, always turning and looking for a better position. Then, at the first hint of light she puts an ankle sock over her eyes."

"Oh," I said, "oh." And that had been that, it had been alluded to, the actual text, the imagining of two women together. My mind separated itself briefly from my brain and journeyed a short distance in none of the four traditional directions. I smiled comfortably, knowing I would leave soon.

Driving back to Calgary, though, I thought, a woman seemed not a bad idea. Why not? I was amazed that I had never thought of it before, as I planned phone calls and assignations with Jackie which never occurred. I talked too much about Jackie to Joel though, I suppose. He thought we were lovers. Well, he was wrong, I can say for once, huffily and with virtue.

But it does bring me to Miranda and the turning of the tables because now it is me who has first noticed the momentum of desire. Ha ha, I thought to myself as we sat together on the beach last night, aware of spin and magnetism and gravity and all of the physical attributes of the universe which I believed to be propelling the two of us along in unobservable and sympathetic ways.

There are boyfriends, too many boyfriends, I admit, the cause of much worry for Jocelyn, and the reason for her plastic bag of toiletries meant to ward off contagion. Jocelyn believes that her mother is sick. "She shares too many men," Jocelyn said to me recently. "She puts them in her bed and I have seen them through they window from here." *The* becomes *they* in Jocelyn's English. We were sitting on the balcony and Jocelyn showed me how she could peer through the window by chinning herself on the ledge. As we looked inside together, at the messy room, I had a sense of Jocelyn's horror at all matters adult, their bigness and their hairiness and their night time noises and violence, and I had compassion for her wish for a separate bag of purity.

The current boyfriend is Maurice, a wan fellow from England with yellow hair which stands up straight, and brown eyes. I question Miranda about him and the others as we walk the streets of Central looking for work for her. She is very ineffective, even equipped with the resumes Charlie and I have helped her to compose, behaving in the downtown offices of law and insurance and banking as if she barely has the time. She verges on being disrespectful and her eyes dart here and there as if she were taking photographs for the purpose of espionage. After speaking to one or another of several managerial types, we go back outside through huge glass doors and down flights of concrete stairs to the imposing lions or gargoyles guarding the entrances to so many establishments here, where Miranda suggests tea or a walk to a nearby jewellery vendor she knows. She tells me stories about her life.

Last night on the beach she said, "I've always thought that some day I will acquire the temperament for the monastic life. But, of course, if there were any entrance criteria at all, which I presume there are, I would be excluded on the grounds of all of them, I guess, I suppose, particularly any details regarding the entire sphere of my past life."

We were sitting on the tatami mats we take with us and as

she talked she placed stones along the edges, as if there were a strong wind threatening to lift them away, which there was not. She said, "Sometimes I think the way the universe is, with the speed of light and so on, that there are theatre chairs out there at a point where God is, so that when we die we're allowed to move faster than the speed of light to the place where the theatre chairs are and we have to sit with God or one of the assistant holy people and watch the light waves as they arrive with all of the incriminating pictures of us. Since there's an eternity, there will be no problem spending the entire sixty or seventy years required to review everything. There would be no fast forward, but plenty of rewind with long pauses, opportunities to explain ourselves. Anyway, this is what I usually think, after I've been particularly unthinking in my behaviour. I intend to say, you know, if you want us to be human then you have to accept the frailties. I learned that kind of talk when I worked in the customer service section of a department store in Darwin."

"The customers didn't really appreciate my pointing out to them that textiles by their very nature shrink and tear and, if they didn't do so, would not be textiles. The spectators out there in the gold filigree theatre chairs might buy it, if they're at all forgiving, but I don't think the Sisters of the Holy Cross or whoever would. Come to think of it, my spiritual resume is as sketchy as my employment one. Besides, I'm not all that contemplative, but I keep hoping that, by the time Jocelyn and Willy are grown up, I'll have taken a turn in that direction. I'm not sure what kind of aptitude a person is expected to have for the spiritual callings. In high school I was advised to go into physiotherapy as a career, but the thought of more schooling didn't appeal to me. I could type, after all."

Miranda stopped talking then, as if all subsequent work and career choices had been explained. We watched the ubiquitous plastic bags roll in and out on sluggish flats of water. It is so heartening to sit on the sand at night, I thought, and to discover that the earth has held on to a portion of the sun's heat, bringing the life of daytime into the evening. Place your cheek next to the sand and there it is, warm breath exhaling.

I said, "Elizabeth told me Hong Kong means fragrant water. And there is a fragrance, not the usual kind of salty smell you get off the coast of Canada."

"I don't know about Canada," Miranda said to me, "but here it smells like the wind. My mother told me – she thinks about the weather, probably too much – she told me that the wind is the most innocent force on earth because it originates out on the water and water is all it has ever known when it reaches the coast, just one element. So I guess the wind blowing above the water can smell of only one thing and that is the fragrance of not knowing anything else, or naivete, maybe."

"Which is kind of like certainty," I added.

She looked at me and shrugged. "You'd have to discuss that with my mother," Miranda said. The water made soft gulping noises as it lapped on to the beach, not much louder than a cup being dipped for a drink.

"The monastic life doesn't appeal to me," I said then, "too much earnestness and too much of the sedentary life. How often do nuns get transferred to another place? Never, I imagine."

We talked and sat on the beach for a long time and I was aware of wanting an easier comfort with Miranda. That's when it really hit me, the attraction, and I suppose that is really not such a disgrace. I wanted to lie next to her in the sun and study the sandy hairs on her arms the way I used to with school friends. But the sun had gone down hours ago, and in the dark I felt her to be slipping away from me into the shade, so before we went home I stood and walked here and there, as if I had some plan, as if looking for a lifeguard or a dog or a certain kind of shell. Which is something I do often. Oh yes, I like to make people think I had intended to do this all along.

RICHARD

Richard was about to listen to an old recording by Glen Campbell and Bobby Gentry. It was a record his father had listened to many times, over and over for a while, and Richard had gotten an urge to hear it again. For days, after work he had looked through the depressing bins of old records at several of the city's secondhand stores and at last had found a copy. The music of the Campbell and Gentry duo had served as a kind of soundtrack for events as they had risen up, it seemed, looking for a soft place to fall. What had been important about the recording owned by Duncan McDonagh was that a scratch existed in one of the tracks, causing the needle to skip and Duncan to believe – in a manner so typical of him, out of a process incomprehensible to everyone else – that it was necessary to stand beside the stereo console and gently press the arm ahead at the critical moment, deftly preventing any disconnections in the music. That was his goal, his insane and preposterous goal, for weeks during that fall after the swim when Elizabeth was living with them.

Richard placed the record on the turntable, cursing the unseasonable cold and the wind outside, and the mess in his apartment. These days Reba had difficulty finding a space to sleep that was not covered in newsprint or photocopies of magazine articles, and the wheeled chair was stuck in a corner of the kitchen behind a very full green garbage bag.

Have I always lived in this quagmire? he wondered, as "Gentle On My Mind" began to play. Have I always been the kind of person whose neighbours will be interviewed by the press when something finally goes wrong, neighbours who prudently state that yes, he stuck to himself and yes, there was something a little bit odd about him, but we couldn't really put a finger on it, until this... this outrage.

No. Hearing the record reminded him that the circumstances of daily living had been acceptable enough for most of his life. As a child, things had been a bit slap-dash at times, with mustard and bologna sandwiches often served for meals, pop-tarts for dessert and, at least twice a week, TV dinners. The position of the television had been a bit unconventional, high up in a corner on a shelf constructed by Louise so that the noon and six o'clock news could be viewed comfortably from the table. In order to change channels, Richard and Gayle had had to scrape a wooden chair across the linoleum floor, and the sound of chair legs on linoleum still aroused in Richard an anticipation of "Bonanza" or "Green Acres."

The stereo had been in the living room, a room that was rarely used except for parties, Christmas or possibly the convenience of the occasional encyclopedia salesmen. Duncan had always treated salespeople with extreme solicitude, helping them to display their products upon the coffee table, shooing everyone else out of the room, listening attentively to sales pitches, all of which infuriated Louise.

That was how things had been most of the time, although Duncan had always had his strange times, his distant times, times when he was not able to sleep, times when he had made plans to switch to sunflowers, reforest, times when he claimed he couldn't make his hands work, and times when he worried about crazy things such as all of the animals' heads being too large. For the most part, though, the circumstances of daily life were not bad. There were just the episodes.

Duncan had bought his Glen Campbell and Bobby Gentry record at a secondhand store as well, a consignment shop in town called Second Time Around. He had never bought a record there before, having only mail-ordered records from an RCA club they belonged to for years. And never had he been a fan of country music; he had always preferred the big band sound. But, how like his father to have nothing unlike him, Richard thought. There had really been nothing fixed when it came to what Duncan McDonagh might or might not have done and so a scratched country and western record from a secondhand store could be considered a perfect bit of logic, he supposed now.

At first Duncan had played the record only in the evenings, after chores. He would sit in the kitchen until the skipping began, then walk indifferently into the living room to tap the needle and return to the kitchen table where everyone else sat, Richard, Gayle and Elizabeth doing homework, and Louise, if she were at home, reading or writing.

Duncan's devotion to the recording deepened. He began listening to it in the mornings as well as at lunch time, rising several bars before the skip to stand over the console, watching the rotating disk, hoping to prevent the jumping, repeating craziness of that one line. Richard came to it now as he sat listening. It was a line from a song called "Sunday Morning" and the scratch had been in the refrain, a line that went "Do what other people do," but with the skip, what Richard and Gayle used to hear was "Do what uh, do what uh, do what uh," until Duncan lifted the needle and the music continued. How strange to hear it play through without a skip, an unexpected relief.

Once Duncan had begun standing by the record player in mute preparedness for this imperfection, Louise took it upon herself to follow him into the living room, questioning the need to play that particular record. As far as Richard knew, Duncan had replied with his total silence, his undivided absence.

To discourage Duncan, Louise had tried reading in the living room while Gayle sat on the floor at the coffee table to do her homework. Both, Richard thought, believed that Duncan's episode could be aborted; if the clan would just gather in, Duncan would stop, reflect carefully and smash the record. This had not happened, of course. He listened to the record more and more, even bought others which also required careful watching. Louise abandoned the living room. Gayle stayed. And Richard remained at the kitchen table, looking out at the aging corn and wondering if he would, at last, have to call the neighbourhood men in to harvest. To have to initiate such grave adult activity had left him sitting with his ruler balanced on his right index finger, swaying ever so dreamily, the way a line in balance will. Louise swore that she would not call them, that Duncan could live with the consequences this time. But it was Elizabeth who finally broke the spell or maybe it was just that the spell was ready to be broken. All she had to ask, one evening, was, "Duncan, why do you like those records so much? What do you see in them anyway?" The next day, he lost interest in the records before the corn had frozen to death. Not long after (it was a bright November morning), the men drove in the laneway with the beaked harvester and the wagons and Duncan McDonagh was right on track again.

Richard sat and stared at the record jacket, feeling much the same way he had back then with his ruler, unable to decide whether to tip this way or that, to undertake a myriad of tasks in a kind of trance of efficiency, or to sit, in the luxurious stupor of the day-dreamer. The dilemma was resolved by the re-discovery beneath the papers, of a tape from Elizabeth which had arrived on Thursday.

"I'll go to the university, to the language lab, this very afternoon. Joel can come along. No, on second thought, I'll go alone and screen it for material he might not want to hear."

Before leaving, Richard performed certain of his new kitchen acts, as he called them. He stirred bran and honey into yogurt and spread marmite on to rye flatbread which scratched his esophagus as it went down. Standing at the sink was the way in which Richard liked to eat on weekends. As he leaned forward in his black housecoat, the motion of his neck and jaw resembled the taut, eager chewing motion of a dog, which was deceiving because Richard did not enjoy this type of food. He would rather have eaten corn flakes or fried eggs, but there were times, and this was one, when he hoped that healthier, less tasty food could assist him in drawing nearer to his goals of comfort and peace. At the same time, he recognized this hope as a form of modern folklore, even modern puritanism, and before tidying up, for no reason other than to mock his fickle approach to diet, decided to immerse a piece of flatbread in a shallow dish of water. He would see just how much it could absorb while he was out, how bloated and disgusting it could become.

With this project undertaken, Richard knew, from the sensation in his soul, that the grim part of his day was over. It was like getting free of a traffic jam and happened every day at about noon. Once the grim part of his day was over, Richard began to feel more kindness toward himself and his surroundings. Even so, he imagined, when down on the sidewalk, that the grey-blinded interior was relieved to have him gone, that the furniture creaked restfully without him and that all of the smaller objects, the pens and papers and so on, settled into their shelves and tables, knowing that no agitated movement would be visited upon them.

It was a pleasure now, to look forward to the transit ride to the university with the other quietly travelling faces. It is like being a baby, Richard thought, having our bodies carefully transported by a gently rocking force. And he was pleased with the possession of a tape-recorded message from Elizabeth and gladdened to be able to feel some excitement. He had not yet dug himself into a newspaper-lined cave. There was not a great likelihood that he would be found just yet in his apartment, dead as a doornail within his unlit labyrinth of print. No, it had not come to that, mercifully.

Richard entered the library, conscious of being a patron rather than an employee, and walked the steps down to the language labs in the basement. The atmosphere was spritely and illiterate downstairs, with the red carpeting and travel posters and tape machines with people listening. Richard often thought he might like to transfer down to this part of the library, where he imagined entire days were passed listening to Bulgarian choral works or watching filmstrips titled *Les Cathedrales de France*.

He located a machine and threaded the tape through. How surprising to have Elizabeth's voice there, ruddy and clear as if she were in the chair next to him. "Hello, Richard," she said. "If you are in the language lab, please swivel around and admire the poster of René Lévesque for me. I always made a point of studying it when I visited the basement for preliminary instruction in Cantonese. Those lessons, by the way, were of limited use although a touch more useful than the Mandarin Self-Taught has been. I cannot seem to progress past lesson three, "Short Sentences." As you might well imagine, the scope of this chapter is almost limitless. Should I master it, I am allowed to move on to chapter four, "Long Sentences," such as 'He has a headache and a fever.'"

Elizabeth talked about the political climate in Hong Kong, the new parties forming as well as the old allegiances of both communists and capitalists. It was not acrimonious there on the island, though, she said, likening the factions to teams, with recognizable uniforms. "There is a group of communist women who all seem to own the same purse," Elizabeth commented, "a black and shapeless vinyl creation. I do not know how it has come to pass that I am considered to be on the communists' team but perhaps it is because of my timeless fashion sense." There was a pause, then Elizabeth added, "I don't really mean to be flippant."

Another silence and then, "This Miranda we are living with is a cultural risk, a cultural liability. It was not wise on my part to move in with her, although I do like her in a way. And I do not like to see the state intervening when children are involved, which they are threatening to do. Only last week a social worker showed up on the doorstep so God knows what type of grievous neglect or inadequacy has been recorded on a file somewhere. She vowed to be more attentive in the future and was contrite and so on in the presence of the social worker, but I am dubious. She does not seem to be able to keep pace with the demands of life. As a result, I am finding myself more and more cast into the role of loans officer for Miranda.

"What she wants to believe, Richard, is that currency is not required in this quaint and rustic island corner of the world. She weaves products for exchange, with no thought of demand. For example, I now own three camera straps and am owed another as Miranda's contribution to the gas bill. Fish soup is another denomination in the economy. It has all become so desperate that I accompanied her on her last trip to the Miramar Bakery to collect child support payments from Gordon, the ex-husband. He is a smarmy fellow, a dentist, obviously very involved with his tan, but nevertheless wanting to discuss the concept of Cartesian doubt amid fulsome warm placements of his hand upon my forearm. He was spending the day in a state of wilful suspension of belief. I interrogated him about his dental practice but he was vague, sailing out in lunatic tacks, zigzagging his way back to the essence of the pastry he was eating. I was wishing Joel could have been there.

"Eventually, Gordon was able to believe that the bills before his eyes—for rent, for groceries, past due at the dentist on the island Miranda takes the kids to out of a spite she will not admit to—were genuine, and we arrived at a figure for the month's expenses, although he balked at the dentist's bill. For next month I will attempt to monitor Miranda's expenses in some way, maybe ask for receipts occasionally, although I do not have the temperament for auditing.

"What is really irritating to me is that I am sure she gives money to the church. They, for some reason, require the actual symbol, the representation of goods on coloured paper as opposed to woven place mats or a calligraphic thought from André Gide. Miranda says she would like to join the Carmelite Order when her children are older. Ha. Total incongruity can be charming when it is not living with you. The boyfriends are a 'celebration,' she says, which is finite. There is a line of candles to be lit but it is growing shorter. Too many dark smoking ones left behind, she tells me.

"Gayle likes her, which I have to admit does not surprise me. It is good to have Gayle here and to find publications such as *The Begoniac* lying around. She is working for a fellow here named Charlie, helping him with his research on book-burning. Yesterday I took her to a favourite spot of mine along the footpath to a village called Tai O. There is a little temple by the waterfront and joss sticks burn perennially and quiet people come and go. Further on is a small outdoor café where we drank beer and ate peanuts from the shell. Gayle wanted to reminisce, but I was not in the mood. Evocations of the time I lived with you are not always my idea of recreation. I still recall everything that went on at your house occurring against a quiet hissing sound. That was fear, I guess; it's like having two seashells clapped against your ears creating a constant washing away of confidence. When Mom finally came back from the hospital, it didn't seem real, and Duncan's leaving so soon after only added to the metaphysical tempest, as if some power were having difficulty being absolute about McDonagh souls in southern Ontario.

"Well, anyway, you probably want an update on the gossip at work, life at the British Council. You remember Rose? Well, now she's moved in with Gavin, and his Polish-born wife and children have gone back to Europe. Gavin is the one who believes that all of the students must be given English names. He has missed several staff meetings recently and no excuse is ever given. Rose's face always seems a bit too pinkish, which is appropriate, I guess."

Elizabeth talked at length about the intrigues at work, knowing Richard's fascination with gossip, even when the characters were completely unknown to him.

"In review then, as we used to say in those tedious early morning seminars I used to attend on Canadian and American history, what have I said? Nothing of substance," Elizabeth concluded. "I am reading a book by V.I. Lenin, a gift from the communists next door. *What is to be Done?* is the title. Isn't it reassuring that one as doctrinaire as he could ask such a plaintive question? I will let you know the answer. Are the mountains still standing? I miss them and you and Joel, but I am still liking it here, and for some reason teaching English to adults in Hong Kong is still more appealing than teaching history to junior high students in Calgary. I'll be in touch again soon. All for now," and there followed that dreadful muffled thump, like someone falling, Richard thought, as Elizabeth disconnected herself.

Richard rewound until the tape tick, tick, ticked in that delicate way associated with the conclusion of civilized and educational events. It reminded Richard of the socialists' meetings he and Elizabeth had attended long ago when Elizabeth was in her final year of university and Richard in his first, where they had watched films of hydro-electric dams being constructed or vignettes of Mao swimming the Yellow River at an advanced age. As the lights used to come on and the sounds of rewinding began and ended, Richard and Elizabeth's eyes would meet in candour and mild embarrassment. The discussions had been replete with words and phrases never heard elsewhere, such as "hegemonists" or "the demise of the ruling class." It was as if the room where they met were a place people congregated to practice speaking in another dialect; there had been the same self-consciousness about it. Still, Richard and Elizabeth had returned month after month, even though Richard complained about the women looking plainer than necessary and Elizabeth could not sit still throughout a meeting and was forever running off to buy fuses or Styrofoam cups.

Richard believed now that that was really where Elizabeth's journey to Hong Kong had begun, back there in the public library in the little university town of Albion, Ontario. It pleased him that there had been a route, a place from which a destination had been sighted and pursued. It could not be condensed and made brief and inscrutable. If Elizabeth were to die tomorrow, the newspapers would not think to include those early passionate times when China and ideology were clasped together with the romantic belief that people could work with one another in absolute unison for the selfless and the abstract and be happy and laugh in small groups around a piece of heavy industry, a turbine perhaps, which all had helped to create after a day in middle school.

The core of what Elizabeth believed, Richard thought, despite the irony in her voice at times, was that the human heart was good and was beating patiently for the correct material circumstances to permit a flooding together, a convivial embrace. That was why she liked other languages, Richard suspected; there was always the possibility that this new voice might open the door to a more roseate species of humanity.

Richard sat for a while, envying Elizabeth. Then he slipped the tape back into its bubble padded envelope and went outside. Down the hill alongside the clamorous and intolerant traffic he walked, then on to the merciful side street, past the school with its Sunday restfulness, to the house where Joel now lived alone. Richard had a longing to see the yard and its trees and flowers; not necessarily Joel.

There was something impatient about the very windows of this house now, without Gayle, and Richard suspected Joel was at home, which he was, in the back yard listening to his radio. In the shade of the two large spruce trees Joel wore a cotton toque, because he did not like his head to be the least bit cool. It was a foolish hat, with a pompom, very white against the low-hanging branches of the spruce and the uncut grass.

Looking up, Joel said, "I'm glad you're here. I was just daydreaming about someone maybe interviewing me."

Richard immediately began to regret his decision to drop by, chastising himself for thinking that he could have seen this yard without an encounter with its owner.

"They interview so many people on the CBC," Joel continued, "and I think I have some things to say that are just as useful as some babe describing a recipe that requires the use of individual ramequins. Do you have any individual ramequins at your house? This person I've been listening to does."

"What are they?" Richard asked.

"I don't have a clue," Joel answered. "They sound like miniature goats."

Joel stood and asked Richard if he would like a beer, went inside and re-appeared seconds later with two bottles and two pair of gloves. "You might want to wear these," he said. "It's cool out here in the shade, but nevertheless I am trying to experience something like early summer. It's the best I can do."

Richard put on Gayle's old, floppy, beige gardening gloves. He was feeling as if he had interrupted Joel in conversation with his yard, as if Joel might have been sitting in his lawnchair talking in the general direction of the perennial border.

"Yes, I've been sitting here, wishing someone would come along and interview me," Joel said, "just give me fifteen or twenty minutes on one of those morning talk shows, not the phone-in variety with the assholes they're always trying to get off the air as soon as they begin, but a real studio interview with someone who is very interested in me, genuinely interested, you know, as if I had just won a major book award or an Olympic gold medal."

"So, what would you say?" Richard asked.

"I don't know. What would you ask?"

"Well, what do you want me to ask?" Richard inquired a little impatiently.

"Ask me if I expected Gayle to leave."

Richard felt overwhelmingly weary. This was a mistake, coming here like this, he thought. But, nevertheless, "OK," he said, "Did you expect Gayle to leave?"

"Thank you," Joel said, shifting positions in his chair. "No, frankly, I did not. I should have, but I did not. So it goes when the organism finally relaxes and lets down its defenses, lies in front of the fire like a contented dog – so it goes. A person should always be on the ready, keep a scrapbook of disaster photos to leaf through now and again, just to keep the adrenalin pumping."

"Now what?" Richard asked.

"Ask me why I should have known."

"This is stupid, Joel."

"Just ask."

"OK. Why should you have known she was planning to leave?"

"The reasons I should have known, you ask? Well, several come to mind now that I have had time to wander my house and yard in the evenings and on weekends. Drinking a lot you might think, but, in fact, no, I drink very little. Nor do I smoke."

Richard's thoughts turned to his own dietary habits and pleasant musings about the flatbread.

"The evidence is as follows," Joel said. "We had been in the house for four years, prior to which I had known Gayle for two years. Six years is a long time, don't you think, and it is a significant amount of time. I know because I have calculated something based upon it. And, I have given some thought to the other people, the other possible lovers, all of whom for some reason lived in British Columbia. The bonsai tree man, that other one who came to visit and even that Jackie woman. Things went on."

"Just as an aside," Joel said, looking directly at Richard, "I know you two were accomplices in these little intrigues. It was inevitable, and, if I have one bit of advice to give the listening audience, it is to stay away from twins. There is something misguided about them. Their loyalty to one another goes too far."

Richard removed the gardening gloves. He did not really wish to be hearing Joel's ideas on misguided loyalties and was about to comment, but Joel carried on with his narrative, changing his tone of voice. The expression beneath the white toque became hangdog. "It's not that the collusion was that important, or any of the indiscretions. I could have disregarded it all. No, it was more that she did not wish to sink down into this place with me. That is what I can see now."

Silence. "Could you ask, 'Meaning exactly?'"

Richard rolled his eyes and sighed. "Yes—all right. Meaning exactly?"

"Well," Joel began, "meaning just that. When I am in my back yard I feel at times so immobilized with ease that I wonder if I have possibly sunk into the lawn right up to my neck, and the funny thing is, it's a very comfortable feeling. You would think a person might be claustrophobic, but no, I feel as if I could be sunk right in, legs crossed, hat on, pleasingly stuck. What I did not suspect, and I should have, is that Gayle did not feel at all that way. She started out feeling that way but then she stopped. And this is the part that you may not believe but I know the exact moment when things changed and that is why the six years is important because it was about halfway through them."

Richard watched Joel carefully, listening in part and at the same time imagining the flatbread filling with water. He pictured it to be like a brown and middle-sized seal, curled up in his sink. "Uh huh," Richard said, without prompting. "Go on."

"We had been living here for one year," Joel said, "from August until August and we had done a lot of work, the garden and the yard and put the hardwood on the living room floor and bought things and I was ready to settle into fall, feeling like a satisfied pilgrim, very happy with this part of the new world, and I said to Gayle, in this very yard, 'Let's have a big Thanksgiving dinner and invite everyone we know and get Lucille to come with her fiddle.' That's the sort of plan I had in mind."

"And Gayle looked at me and that was the moment. It was as if she had been diving down to roost here like a cormorant or any of those birds that can come out of a nose dive and that's what she did. She came right out of that dive. That look, the expresion on her face – it was very still but it was as if there were feathers all around her and a backward, skidding action, and she said, 'No, let's go somewhere. Let's go somewhere for the long weekend.' And that was that. We went to Winnipeg to see Greg and Mary. So the point is, you see, not so much the infidelities, but the betrayal way back then, the betrayal of intentions, the giving up on the future."

Richard was silent, having no consolation to offer but wondering if, before Gayle left, all of his interaction with Joel had been like this. No, he thought, there had been conversations. Richard could recall several on the topics of politics and Joel's colleagues and they had laughed and talked and there had been nothing particularly satanic about his alliance with Gayle. She had not required de-programming in order to take off on her own to Hong Kong.

A cool breeze blew through the yard, causing Joel to pull his hat down over his ears. "You are becoming as fucked as me," Richard thought of Joel, wondering why he continued to see someone this unpleasant. "Why do I not socialize with people who thrill at the sight of me? or at least reach for a softball to toss, or a basketball, rather than insults to hurl at my only sibling."

Richard answered himself frankly. "It's because you have no other friends," he admitted, and joined Joel in staring at the perennial border.

"What do you think about going camping on the long weekend?" Richard asked after a while.

"What, you, me and Sandra, you mean?"

"No, just you and me. I haven't seen Sandra for three or four weeks. I'm kind of holed up right now, incommunicado. I can't even reach my telephone without tipping over a little bit in my rolling chair. Anyway, I've been thinking about camping. I know a little municipal place down in Crow's Nest. The Canada Day crowd wouldn't be there."

"OK," said Joel. "Sure. Why not?"

Richard finished his beer and left. He spent the walk home thinking that it had been a mistake to ask Joel to go camping, kicking himself for it, regretting the entire visit. The only good that had come of it was that it had provided his flatbread the opportunity to absorb the utmost amount of water. He could hardly wait to get home to see it.

Gayle

Today we had a hot fog. I did not realize such a weather condition was possible, but in places such as this Hong Kong archipelago, it apparently is. There can be a hot fog hanging above the water. I could see it from the balcony in the early morning; then, I passed through it myself later on. There were even portions of hot fog scudding along the street below.

Only Elizabeth seems able to enjoy this heat and humidity. Toward afternoon, as everyone becomes more and more dispirited, dank like their clothing and the too close sky, she contentedly plans her English lessons at the table in the hallway. One silver fan circulates the air around Elizabeth, across her shoulder and the back of her neck. From time to time she goes to it and stands with her face or a wrist or an armpit to the propelled air.

Elizabeth must plan diligently these days, as she is now the only wage earner. My income from Charlie is negligible and Miranda has only scanty bits of unreliable work, teaching English. Many days she sails into the city, tramps through the streets of Wanchai or rides the bus to disreputable looking offices in Aberdeen to find that the student has cancelled. At least, that is what she says. Sometimes she returns with Maurice, from the hostel.

Despite the economic situation here, Elizabeth does not object to Maurice's presence. I think, for her, the word hostel is the equivalent of chaos. Elizabeth envisages stooped figures in undershirts stepping over and upon muddled sleeping bags in search of misappropriated toiletries. She probably imagines insufficient light and rapidly decaying teeth and is, therefore, somewhat relieved for Maurice when he can spend time with us, in a place that is well lit and ventilated, where personal hygiene is easily organized.

I, on the other hand, find Maurice an aggravation – his thinness, his manner of speaking, his hair, but, most of all, his occasional presence in the morning. Miranda and the children go off to mass every morning – she is serious about this Catholicism – leaving me with Maurice. He rises early and waits for coffee to be made. I believe he stands outside my door, listening for me. He waits for me to buy the paper. He sits on the balcony and awaits an offer of eggs or fruit, or he asks if he can borrow a few *renminbi* for *congee* from the stall in the street. He thinks that to say *renminbi* for dollars is clever. My teeth grate, and I delight in saying, when I can, "Sorry, Maurice. I haven't been to the bank."

I have taken to going to a little café on the mornings Maurice is here to read the paper and to drink my coffee because I cannot endure his yellow-haired attentiveness. It's as if he is a bird-watcher and I am the watched bird, expected at any moment to display a rare ritualistic dance of generosity. If only he would sleep in like Elizabeth does, but no, his metabolism is more efficient than most, he claims. Only four hours of sleep a night are necessary. This morning, to my relief, I had the excuse of going into the city to read with Charlie and take notes, and Maurice was left behind, alone on his balcony aerie, disappearing into the fog.

One of Charlie's many good qualities is that he can be counted on to be silent in the mornings. We sat on the lower deck in the open air, thoughtful, pulling our clothing from our arms and legs, and I became mesmerized by the effect of the rising sun on the fog and the water. I was reminded of that book of Lennart Nilsson's photographs Dad gave me for Christmas long ago. The colours of this morning had the same pinkish-white look and swirl as the entrance to the fallopian tubes, if I remember correctly, only enlarged again and again, so that today we were able to travel by boat into those gossamer channels. I had to keep telling myself, it's radar that will get us to the main land, not the pull of reproduction.

It was the last Christmas we had together that Dad bought that book for me. I can still see so clearly the taste buds and the hairs that looked like a forest of aspens, and staphylococci in cavernous pores. And there were the empty chambers of an infant's heart, so clean and unabraded, as I guess all of our hearts are, at first.

There was a period of time after that Christmas, when Dad and I used to sit in the living room after chores and look through that book together. I remember being jealous of the time, hoping Richard would stay upstairs reading, hoping that no one would come along and interrupt. We conducted almost the same conversation, night after night; it came to be like a recitation or a script.

"Hard to believe they have no eyes," I always said of the sperm circling an egg, all facing it like blind tadpoles.

And Dad would say, "They're guided by hormones."

On the following page the sperm spun the egg with their tails and I always felt a dizzying helplessness at that point and said, "Reminds me of being turned and turned in a game of blind man's bluff."

Dad's response was, "I suppose it's a bit like a game. The chromosomes are looking for a partner."

It struck me this morning that neither of us was at all shy about the content of those photographs. I guess there is a point at which, through magnification, intimacy becomes transformed into something generic and material. Although, at the time, for my eleven-year-old mind, all of that white and flowing motion, all of that predestiny, reminded me more of weddings than biology. Especially those velvety, beckoning fallopian tubes.

"Off they go," I would say of the zygote, "behind the curtains."

"They know exactly where to go now, and what is necessary to survive," Dad used to say in reply.

I was drifting along in a half-sleep this morning. Charlie had gone to stand on the deck, he had disappeared from view and all around me was the pinkish fog, with dark bits of red here and there, the sun, or maybe blood, I thought, and the smell of salt water.

I must have been under the influence of colour this morning, the red and pinks in particular, because that sky reminded me of another time after that Christmas, Valentine's Day. I remembered it being late afternoon, dark already, and I was studying the valentine that had been given to me by Donny Creighton. He had added a row of x's and o's and I was flattered but at the same time worried about the genuineness of this message. He did not seem to have pressed very hard with the pen, I thought; the x's and o's had an ambiguity about them and I wondered if Donny had written them on a dare. That was when Mom called Eva Ferguson to tell her that Dad was off again. And that time, I recall disliking her use of the word, talking as if Dad were meat that had gone bad, oily and blue-tinted, drawing us all to look closely, but breathe sparingly, in his presence.

But, of course, she was right. He was off. That was one of the times Dad stopped talking for several days and complained of a weakness in his hands, saying he could not do up the snaps on his jacket. Richard and I milked the cows, leaving him to feed the calves, but even that was too much. Holding the pail against those butting heads was like pushing against the elements for him, trying to stave off spring. Instead, he would comb away the cows' winter coats while we worked and Mom canvassed the countryside for the New Democrats.

It was startling when he finally came around one evening. I think he had helped Elizabeth with some homework, then he came to us and said, "Come on out to the barn, to the hay mow."

So Richard and I followed him out to the barn and up the stairs to that one mow he kept loose, no sharp, shorn grasses wrapped into bundles, just clover and alfalfa; the names are like oriental spices or the moons of a distant planet. Dad sat in the hay and I could tell right away that he was becoming teary-eyed and for no reason at all which made me furious, and lonesome too. I climbed up the cliff of bales and began jumping into the hay near him, and soon Richard was jumping too, and I guess in some fashion we must have bestirred him because after that there was a change. Sometimes it was as if that were all he needed, a jostling.

Dad began to talk again then, even did some canvassing with Mom, joking, as the results came in on election night, "She might have done better if I had stayed at home."

That was the night the kitchen was filled with Mom's supporters and she gave her speech, so like her ("I guess coming in third is better than not coming in at all"), and we all cheered, for both of them, they looked so happy, red-cheeked with excitement like children. Funny to think they were both in their fifties.

Such were my thoughts as I sailed along this morning and such was the daze I was in, for the longest time, until I heard Charlie saying, "Your mouth is open. Your mouth is open." He likes to comment on such situations as mouths being open, breasts being large, toupees being too apparent, or ankles being stout, as he puts it. I closed my mouth and we sailed on very slowly in the heat and the mist. The reds and pinks had bled themselves white and we were out in the South China Sea with nothing but diesel fumes and diesel racket. I became anxious to arrive.

"Shouldn't be more than ten minutes," Charlie answered when I asked how much longer, and he was correct.

When we reached land, the sun broke through, although the oppressive heat remained. Fortunately, the university library seems to have been constructed for maximum circulation of air. The ceilings are high and fans beat above the long oak tables. Blinds billow in the occasional breeze, causing the students to look up, longingly, wishing to fly out and above the pressures of the atmosphere and study.

Charlie had me reading about papal bulls and Rabelais and absolution from ecclesiastical censure, as well as photocopying brief documents and the proceedings from conferences held in Lisbon and Prague. After two hours of this labour, I told him that I needed some air and went out for a walk. It is my habit to do so.

Outside, as is also my custom, I made attempts to ask the grounds crew questions which were not, as they never are, understood, evoking responses which were equally mystifying to me. I asked about soil mix; they answered by showing me the roots of a rhododendron. The exchange of information was satisfactory to all of us.

A little further on, beneath the huge banyan tree, I split open one of the blackish-purple fruits and watched spellbound as four sugary insects emerged. How handy, to spring fully grown from a fig. I considered how comfortable it might be to grow and develop within the trunk of a tree for thirty years, my vascular system spliced together with the cadmium layer so that I could suck away on sugar and develop at least a secondhand relationship with photosynthesis.

Then I lay down and began to wonder if Miranda might have some occasion to be at the university. I watch for her often these days, and have internal conversations with her which sometimes cause my lips to move or a hand to lift as I make a point. I must admit to a mirthfulness in my abdomen. I expect something from Miranda: I am expecting.

I lay there, watching closely the separate leaves of the lawn and the small circuses of insect life. And the grass was sweaty, and I wanted to dig my fingers into the earth and perhaps touch just one blade of grass with my tongue. There were very few students to be seen, so I drew closer to the ground, one hand near my mouth, and very slowly pressed myself into the earth's dampish hair, imagining that it had pressed back, that I could cup my hands around behind and pull it closer.

Then there was Charlie approaching, his green suitcase filled with books and his sandals clapping as they always do. I sat up very quickly, lines of grass imprinted on my cheek and a bit of green stuck in the corner of my mouth. I wanted to begin an explanation, feeling exposed, an object of lurid fascination, like the mating dogs I saw recently, stuck together in the market place, trying to disengage as people watched, warming with curiosity about animal pleasure.

I had to say something quickly, so I asked Charlie if he owned a slide projector and yes, he does, and yes, I may borrow it. He was in a rush to catch the ferry and was talking too quickly and I was not listening at all, only watching, when I could, the red lips behind the mustache. I wanted to ask him exactly what he thinks of Miranda. Not everyone adores her, after all. There is even outright ridicule of her hat in the village and talk about her boyfriends, and whenever the propane man sees her, he wails Cantonese invective and spit forms in the corners of his mouth. It is hatred in the fourteen tones I understand exist in the language.

And the children are too often fed pastries and moved from the bedroom to accommodate lovers. "Can the kids sleep in your room tonight?" Miranda will ask, as Maurice sits beneath his yellow hair-mop. Or, I will arrive home from an evening with Charlie and Pui Sin to find them in my room, heads at opposite ends of their narrow mattress, or Jocelyn, cocoon-like in a cotton sheet on the floor.

I buy Jocelyn and Willy mangoes and bananas and insist that they eat them, and I counsel Miranda to buy specific grains and vegetables. Her paleness suggests to me a need to be fed the darker and brighter foods, tomatoes and snow peas and black beans. Still, I must say in her defense, that there is the loom, which is steadfast and speaks of Miranda's potential for discipline and work and temperance. When she sits and weaves amid the disorder of our living room we all, even Elizabeth, come to watch, wanting to approve and to see the designs take shape. Richard might like her. I suspect Charlie does not though, so I withheld my question. Later, he asked me to come visit this evening.

The street noises are picking up now because people are coming home and supper is being made and the televisions have been turned on. I think I shall walk through the fields to Charlie and Pui Sin's house now. She and I weed the garden together in the evenings, which I enjoy, while Charlie sits beneath the tarpaulin he has strung up as protection for his lawn chairs and TV tables from the sun and the rain.

Pui Sin told Charlie she is pleased that I do not try to speak mangled Cantonese to her. And she does not speak to me in English. We are completely silent. I crouch between the rows of vegetables or I sit wordlessly beneath the tarpaulin, and at these times I notice that I am filled with waiting. I am a waiter who wants to wait more, to put off and put off. I know I must talk to Elizabeth, but at the same time, I can pump in more and more delay, more and more anticipation, until I have a surplus of it which at times stretches my senses taut, like the tarpaulin, that sighs and carries on above our heads.

Richard

Richard knew that there were people who might consider him to be too reserved; he knew that he was not inclined to dramatic behaviour. Like many people, though, he was attracted to those who were; young men who smashed bare hands through windows in a jealous rage, or women who threw drinks at companions in crowded restaurants. Even motorists who shouted "Get a license" or "Eat shit" caught Richard's attention from the sidewalks he so often walked. Occasionally, he would memorize an angry driver's license plate and watch for it for days afterward.

Only once that he could recall had Richard acted upon impulse. It had happened during a time when he was involved with a woman named Joanne. Richard and Joanne had been a couple, as the concept existed in Richard's mind, for two years, until one evening when Joanne began questioning what she called "the nature of our relationship." She had begun reasonably enough, with a query regarding their future and, much to Richard's amazement, within a matter of minutes, had progressed to a string of accusations.

"You're an emotional cripple," she had said. "You can't communicate. You don't know the meaning of the word intimacy." And so on. Joanne had continued in this manner for at least twenty minutes, after which she had run down the stairs and into her car which Richard could clearly remember fish-tailing away on Memorial Drive.

He had called a cab to give chase, arrived at her apartment and rung the buzzer, but to no avail. When another occupant arrived, Richard sneaked in behind, impressed with his ability to break and enter, and knocked on Joanne's twelfth-floor door, even half-shouted her name a couple of times. Small, yappy-voiced apartment dogs began to bark from behind closed doors and the woman in the place next to Joanne had threatened, also from behind her door, to call the police. From further down the hall had come the voice of a man with an eastern European accent, clear as a bell, as if he had got down on all fours in order to yell through the keyhole, "Get lost, you crazy guy. Hey, crazy guy, take off."

The thing that Richard was struck by that night was all of the timid intensity tucked away inside so many little addresses. They had probably imagined him a muscle-bound marauder, an enraged and tatooed fellow, out for blood. This image delighted him and by the time he arrived home, after a two mile walk, Richard had still felt elated from the experience. And, that had been the end of Joanne.

Taxi chases and the like had not become a pattern for Richard, however, and so he was surprised by his desire to smash, or at least tear, something when Joel called to say that he had asked a woman named Nora to join them for the weekend. It was not only that she was accompanying them, but also that she, this Nora, could not leave until Saturday morning. She was a social worker and she was on call. There was a family in crisis.

"As if she could make a diference," Richard said to himself, picturing a woman in a denim skirt and Birkenstock sandals hoping to rescue two or three generations of con artists and petty embezzlers from themselves, hoping to talk them into at least some system of orderly payment of their debts. "Ha!" Richard said to Reba.

Instead of shredding any of his valuable clippings or hurling his collection of old *Unity Informers* through a window, though, Richard rolled his chair to the fridge for some ice and soda, then to the cupboard where the scotch was kept. It was Friday night, Canada Day weekend. They were supposed to be leaving. Gayle would never have held them up in this way; crises did not occur in the ornamental plant families. Most likely this family in crisis had already left town themselves, Richard thought, hauling a tent trailer soon to be backed into the camping spot which should have been theirs.

He took a sip of his drink. The street sounds were dry, as they should be in summer, and through his window Richard heard bits of music from passing radios, a saxophone and then electric violins. The traffic, and the scotch, were soothing to him. He imagined the stream of cars heading south and west into the foothills to be travelling with the softness and the pulse of pigeons, homing to mysteriously chosen places in the countryside.

Gazing out at the traffic, Richard asked himself why he would expect Joel to be loyal to Gayle. They were not twins, after all, he knew, and he contemplated the likelihood of twinship versus the likelihood of two unrelated individuals meeting. There was no law of probability against which the two events could be compared, so Richard derived satisfaction from likening Joel and Nora to two bits of ragtag newsprint about to be smashed together against a snow fence somewhere. With him and Gayle, there had at least been a biological basis to their connection. They had been there for the DNA and the helixes.

"Misguided loyalties, my ass. There's just a bit more substance to it," Richard said to the cradled telephone receiver.

He decided to watch television and read the paper. The "Brieflies" were a disappointment, but on the science page Richard found an interesting little piece about a huge collection of galaxies astronomers at Cambridge had discovered; the Great Wall, they were calling it and it made no sense to them at all. They were having difficulty fitting it into their three-dimensional map of the heavens, and it shocked and personally irritated Richard that something could not be contained by infinite space. He went to bed in a foul mood.

In the morning, though, Richard was ready and waiting when

Joel and Nora arrived. And, Richard had to admit to himself that within minutes of having met Nora, despite his preconceptions, he was somewhat smitten by her. She seemed to him to be of the sort who is dazzlingly free of anxiety, someone who would always be at ease in her own home, and the homes of others. Richard's only, and superstitious, reason for believing this was that Nora's hair, in the heat and dampness of summer, was charged with electricity. It was the hair of a toddler, so fine that it buzzed upward from her shoulders and clothing, as if it were January or one of the other cold and arid prairie months. But it was not. It was July and thank God for that, Richard thought.

Before they had arrived at the city limits, Nora turned to Richard in the back seat, settled in with the still unrepaired television set, and said, "You're awfully quiet, Richard. I hope you're not... unhappy with the fact that I'm not Gayle." The word unhappy was delivered with such delicacy, it seemed to Richard as if Nora had managed to unfold that word and string it before Richard's eyes to prevent him actually having to hear it. Was this what social workers did? he wondered.

"No, no, not at all," Richard began. "I realized a long time ago, I think it was when I entered first grade, that not everyone could be my twin sister. I'm really very happy that you are who you are." Playfully delivered comments, such as his last one, substituted nicely for sincerity, Richard had discovered over the years.

Nora said, "Well, I want you to know that Joel and I are buddies. That is what we are and that is all. Just in case there is any question. That's what we all could be, buddies. We three could be a scout troop, heading off in a state of... preparedness."

Richard smiled.

"So relax, Richard," Nora said in a way that suggested she knew about his goal, his inability to be at ease in his own home, and Joel's car, and how unlikely it was that he could ever relax, truly, knowing that the days of the year represented an endless number of newspapers dotted with brief documentations of bizarre and untimely accidents and deaths.

Nora had brought along some tapes for which Richard was grateful and they listened to Van Morrison for a while until Joel began a description of a colleague of his who was about to be fired for conducting import-export deals over his office phone.

Several calls to Spain and Mexico had been charged to Alberta Mental Health and three crates of ceramic roosters had been delivered to his office on Friday afternoon. Joel usually found examples of people thinking they might get away with criminal behaviour very amusing. "They think everyone else is really stupid," he said. "They think we are all wandering around in a catatonic daze. They think no one takes notice of anything. What they don't recognize is that there are hordes of people out there who are very interested in details, all kinds of details, like telephone bill details and absence from work details and so on. For every little corner of your existence there is a corresponding person who is interested. People who do stupid crimes don't know that."

They stopped and bought coffee and ice cream bars and drove on, discussing jobs from which they had been fired. Then they talked about supervisors they had hated, in restaurants and bars and factories and at summer camps for children with mental handicaps. In time they arrived at the campground and it was unbelievable, they all took turns saying out the open window of Joel's car, unbelievable that so few sites were occupied. Such broadcast agreement caused them to want a celebratory drink so, as they erected their tents, Nora and Richard drank wine and Joel drank a Gatorade.

They hiked to an alpine meadow where Joel wandered here and there, examining the already dried plant life. It had been an almost rainless spring. He wore an ear warmer beneath his baseball cap. Nora was concerned that Richard might be a vegetarian; she had brought hamburgers for dinner.

"A lot of people are awfully worried about what they put inside themselves. At work there's a group who despair every time they enter the cafeteria. 'What is there here that I could possibly eat?' they simper. They need to make a very public display of their very private and particular appetites. I can't stand smugness," Nora said, whipping the grass with a branch she had carried with her as they walked. "That's one thing about Joel, not a hint of smugness. He's a bit of an oddball, but not a snob. All this stuff to do with body chemistry, the Gatorade and so on and the tryptophan capsules to promote sleep – he's told me about them, that's how I know, just so you don't make any incorrect inferences. Although I guess I can excuse a bit of voodooism in the face of heartache."

Trying to steer the conversation away from heartache and back to diet, Richard said, "I go through periods of time when I buy food I think I should, you know. Grains and seeds and plain yogurt from the Satori Co-op. I sprout beans in a jar in my tea towel drawer. I spread marmite on toast. Then I get infestations of merchant grain beetles. I'm experiencing one right now actually. I have to throw it all out and swab my cupboards down with an insecticide called Malanox. 'Have a bad night,' I figure it means. I can't seem to stick with the Satori plan for very long."

Richard became aware of Nora's inattention. Her eyes were fixed on Joel, and Richard was reminded of a girl he had known and liked in high school – Rachel Nesbit was her name – of the many times he had spoken to her while her eyes had searched behind him for someone else who should have stopped at her locker instead. But it did not matter; Richard experienced a boozy warmth toward Nora anyway.

She lay on her back and began to sing "Jamaica Farewell" and Richard realized that Nora did want his attention, but in a non-specific way, as a pair of eyes and ears, as an audience. It occurred to him that this was a very satisfactory arrangement after all, absolutely suited to him, really, and he lay down as well. Joel joined them and they listened to Nora's voice, faint ribbons of song being whisked away on the wind.

After a while, Joel said, "I suppose it's the lack of oxygen in this mountain air that causes a person to feel so peaceful. Less for the hemoglobin to carry; less for the brain to work with."

"I would think that in this air," Richard said, "there would be more oxygen, more than in Calgary, anyway. And besides, don't you think you feel peaceful just because it is peaceful here? Couldn't we have a simple reason for today?"

"Yes, certainly we could have a simple reason," Joel said, a bit of satire in his voice. "Like, for example, I won a hockey pool at work last winter and I am still happy, no – jubilant – about that. Two hundred and fifty dollars it was. Or, it might be because I saw Dr. Hoffman, my old advisor, in a restaurant last week and I told him that I had had an article accepted by the *Journal of Nervous and Mental Diseases*, and he slapped me on the back and said 'Way to go!' I could be at peace because of that event, but then again my peace could be disturbed by wondering why I still care about his approval this many years after my thesis defense."

God, this man needs something, Richard thought, a drink maybe, a good fuck, maybe some type of medication. "Could be the lead emissions in the Calgary air," Richard said, "slowing you down, dragging on that hemoglobin like little anvils, hampering the speed of your thinking and your development."

Joel laughed, then coughed, and then asked Richard and Nora if that happened to them very often, "a laugh turning into a cough, I mean," he said. "I wonder if it means anything."

When evening came they built a fire and fried hamburgers and toasted buns. They ate and watched the fire as campers will do and heated water for the dishes while Nora puttered around with a travel alarm clock she had. She was setting it for 4 a.m. so that she could rise and catch a glimpse of the night creatures, she said, the owls in particular.

Joel and Richard sat up with the fire. Joel said he could not recall the last time he had sat in darkness. He said that he liked, recently, to be bathed in electric light and electric sound and proposed that maybe that was why he needed Gatorade, to neutralize all of those photons absorbed sitting in his bright living room. He decided to have one beer, just one beer, from the cooler and as he sat down again he said, "You know, if it weren't for the ambiguity of the situation with Nora, this could almost be considered the perfect circumstance, as Gayle used to say."

"Gayle told you about that stuff, did she?" Richard asked. "It was always a good sign when we could discuss the perfect circumstance at home. It meant that Dad was in an up phase. Did she tell you that we used to invent perfect circumstances for different members of the community as well? Bernice Hanna, for example, owner of the dress shop, Vanity Fair, who pronounced detergent with the emphasis on the first syllable, as in det'ergent," Richard said, then repeated, "det'ergent. We used to have her in the A & P surrounded by grocery store employees, all speaking with the emphasis on the first syllable of every word. We would carry on conversations in that way and Mom used to laugh. She never liked Bernice Hanna; she thought she was affected. And not only that, her prices were too high."

"So, what about you and Gayle? Gayle's never really told me any details about your perfect circumstances," Joel said.

"Well, I remember a time when my perfect circumstance was about underground passageways. I had been reading about the tunnels in Akron, Ohio, the ones used to transport oats, and an explosion that had occurred there, sending a geyser of oats into the air. I kind of liked that idea of things going on and going wrong not too far beneath the earth's surface. So, that was my perfect circumstance, crawling through a manhole into a maze of pipes and tunnels and underground canals, with a flashlight, of course, hoping for an explosion that would send me up to the sky."

"I guess if Gayle had had a perfect circumstance at that time," Joel said, "it did not involve long range plans for living with a man in Calgary who liked to mow his lawn in neat diagonals."

"They never were about the future, Joel," Richard answered, trying to sound kindly. "I can't recall any of Gayle's, offhand, but being here does remind me of one of Dad's, although his were more like reveries than circumstances. When he talked sometimes we would all get the feeling that Dad had slipped under the water like he used to do, and was swimming around in his own private circumstance, that was pretty exclusive."

"It's because we're camping that I've thought of it. He started out talking about the mantle in a lantern, how it could change so suddenly from a white light to just a collapsed bit of grey. And then I think he went on to say that there were times when he was with some of the other men in the community, Alan Porter or Jim Malcolm or any of the others who helped with the harvest and came to play cards in the winter, that there were times when he wished that there were some kind of... evidence is the word he used, I think. Something like the mantle in a lantern, some kind of webbing, that could be seen hooking them all together, even if it were only for a second before it all fell apart. He didn't care. It would be the ideal thing, even if it only lasted for a minute."

Joel asked, "Did he ever just come right out with it and admit that he was lonely?"

"No, not to us. And we certainly never asked. We didn't know what he was talking about, although maybe Mom did. But she was tired of him by then. I imagine she probably turned on the news that night and Gayle and I went to bed. Elizabeth and Dad got along in a kind of way. When she was staying with us, they used to stay up late and talk sometimes when Dad was feeling good."

Joel was silent for a while. He threw a log on the fire and poked at it with a stick and said, "Hmm. Well, I'm glad we can't turn on the news here."

There was the smallest fragrance of snow on the air and the trees had become a black moss against the mountains, containing so many secretive and wild lives. Could the bears and coyotes hear their voices and were they warned to circle even further away? Richard wondered. Their mysterious lives were compelled along their courses by such subtleties as that, or the faintest scent of blood, or a change in the force of the wind. The way things should be, Richard thought, the way things should be.

Richard took the flashlight to the nearest pump where he washed his hands and face in water so cold he had to shake his fingers to warm them, the way people will after cleaning their headlights with snow. When he returned, Joel was brushing his teeth, spitting white foam beneath the branches of a juniper bush. They both fell asleep in their tents before the fire had even begun to die.

Gayle

Already it is the middle of July. Five flag stamps and one of a wolverine now adorn my wall. They are a reminder each morning of how little I have accomplished here.

I began yesterday by walking to Charlie's to borrow his slide projector, which is now in my room, atop the Pepsi crate which houses the slides. I await an evening when I am assured of solitude to view these pictures. Miranda, the children, popcorn, Elizabeth and so on are not what I have in mind.

Then, it being Saturday, I went for a walk with Jocelyn. It seems that the extreme heat and humidity are beginning to leave. Today there was actually a freshness to the wind as if the May breezes had returned, but having had all of the history sieved out, caught in a net over the Indian Ocean. We walked the path to the monastery, then veered off to a spot where we could see the sampans and the neighbouring islands. Jocelyn took out of her pocket a little white card with tiny illustrations of hands, positioned this way and that. "The Deaf Alphabet" it read on the front, and on the reverse side, "Thank you for your support."

Jocelyn studied the card and imitated the hand postures while I lay on my back, observing the sky and thinking that the next time I go into the city I should buy a book of cut-out dolls for Jocelyn. There is a very specific pleasure associated with cut-out dolls that I believe has to do with perfection of fit and congruence. The satisfaction of folding the tabs in such a way that the clothing lies evenly over the flawless underwear, is absolute.

Jocelyn said, "Wash, wash," in her shy voice, meaning watch. Propping the tiny card against a stone, she spelled her name, then mine, then lay down with her head upon my stomach. It occurred to me that Jocelyn's narrow face often seems to be a likeness, or an impersonation, of a child; she looks more adult than eight-year-old.

We had gone walking with the hope of locating Miranda, and as we lay there she appeared, in the distance, approaching from the monastery. Miranda is recognizable by her gait, which is most like a wobbling along the surface of the earth. Jocelyn sat up but did not move to greet her mother, afraid of contamination as she is.

"Now Maurice," she said, in an aggrieved manner. "There was Kim and Ian and Roger." Jocelyn pronounced their names with a laborious pause between each as she spelled it with her fingers. Little did these men know that they would be commemorated in such a way. "There were more than those," Jocelyn concluded as her mother drew nearer.

"I know," I said, trying to be a comfort, "there are people who criticize your mother." Evidently liking the English on her tongue, Jocelyn repeated the word, "criticize, criticize, criticize," until it began to sound to me like the name of a grain or a new strain of water lily.

Miranda was not wearing her hat and the long, black braid was pinned into a coil which leaned to one side of her head. "It's cream," she said, carrying a bottle, holding it out to us as if it were a bird or a large and unusual insect she had caught. "I bought it from one of the priests, actually helped him skim it off myself, with a metal cup. It's easy. The milk below was so watery and blue. It reminded me of Willy's skin when he was born. He was so unhealthy for the first few months. And is he around or is he off with that crowd of juvenile delinquents he calls friends?"

Jocelyn answered in Cantonese, displaying the alphabet card to her mother while reaching into Miranda's pocket for a coin. She took off for the village immediately, leaving the two of us to observe the little messages of dust left behind by her feet. Something auspicious about the way the dust could be supported by the air, I thought later, trying to create a design to what she had done, some necessity.

Miranda sat next to me, her hair more askew that it had appeared from a distance. There were two chopsticks intended to hold it in place, but instead having the effect of heaving the entire bundle downward. It is difficult not to meddle with such asymmetry.

There were no preparatory thoughts to what I did, only Jocelyn's dust and Miranda's comment about watery, blue skin. Kneeling behind her, I took the chopsticks and the pins from her hair, and it was as if all of my muscles felt a relief, changing position from a precarious tilt to flat ground, and so I continued, unbraiding the hair which seemed to cause an equal unfastening of laces in my arms and legs. I combed her hair with my fingers, enjoying the sensation of hair unmanaged after it has been pinned and twisted. That is when I kissed the top of her head, then sat back expectantly, like a dog, waiting for something to occur, although I am not sure what. An immediate conjunction of souls perhaps, or our bodies fitted together like the continents, prior to the Gondwana land drift.

Instead, there was an unhurried moving away, not far, not startled. To a more comfortable position, I told myself, drier ground, slightly elevated so that she could question me. As for me, I felt the pleasant dive of vertigo that accompanies the knowledge of safety.

Miranda looked at me with an expression reminiscent of my old high school nurse, asking me about my period, my bleeding, my cramps. She had a medical curiosity about my behaviour, she had a checklist of questions to ask.

"Are you inclined toward lesbianism?" Miranda asked.

"Well, I wouldn't call it that," I answered.

"What would you call it?"

"An interest," I said. I could feel red blotches appearing on my neck.

"Have you ever gone to bed with a woman?" Miranda asked.

"Not in the flesh."

"Are there alternatives to the flesh that I might not be familiar with?" Miranda asked. "I'd like to know about them. It could save me a lot of trouble."

"Well, there's the imagination," I said, feeling slightly limp and irresolute.

"Yes, there's the imagination," Miranda agreed, and then asked, "and is that satisfactory to you?"

Her voice had such an empirical quality to it that I could not stop myself associating it with the school nurse and the cramps interview of so many years ago. The nurse had seen dozens of girls like me, complaining of cramps and skipping classes. Still, she had managed to sound sincere when she asked if the aspirin had helped. "It still kind of hurts," I said way back then. "It feels like a bone pushing onto muscle. It won't give up."

But to Miranda I said, "No, the imagination is not entirely satisfactory," and we smiled at one another. There was a silence which was not onerous, filled as it was with the moistest of air, as if our thoughts could have been condensed onto the weeds and grasses.

"I've often wondered about nuns," Miranda said, looking out to the water. I followed her gaze, having an immediate impression of nuns engaging in stunts, acrobatics and gymnastics on the beach, seeming to be young killer whales in the water.

"Yes," I replied. "I've wondered too."

And that was all that was said on that topic. I stood and looked at the top of Miranda's head, where it had been kissed, as if I now owned that portion of her hair and skull, as if that were my little bit of territory. Silliness, isn't it?

We walked back into the village and Miranda told me that she was planning to go into the city for dinner with Maurice, and asked if I would mind seeing that the kids were fed. "I don't mind at all," was my response and at that moment I did not. Nor did I later on.

Jocelyn and Willy and I bought a pot of hot and sour soup from the restaurant below our apartment. We had fruit salad made with pieces of coconut, real coconut which we smashed on the floor with Elizabeth's hammer. We lit candles and spread our only tablecloth upon the table, and ate with the transistor playing for us. We went for a walk by the water, where the lifeguards were sitting in their shelter still, playing cards and talking. Further on, we came to the three men in black suits who habitually drink tea on the beach and watch for the ferry to drift in. And when the engine on the nine o'clock ferry cut, I realized that each of the evening's events had been illuminated in my mind and placed on a staircase of mounting hope for Miranda's arrival. She was not on that boat, however.

After eleven, Elizabeth came home, alone, on the final sailing, all full of life and wanting to chat and have a drink with me. All I could concentrate on was that Miranda had stayed overnight in the city without her children. I went to bed wondering where she would sleep, with whom and so on. It was a bit like the bone pushing onto the muscle used to be.

I fell asleep and slept through the night though, dreaming the dream I sometimes have about light, too bright light, the intruding and military kind that searches and sweeps in fearful arcs. Awakened early by this dream, I walked out into the just brightening streets and toward the hills which in the morning are particularly soft and settled in, and I wondered about this business of light. Photosynthesis is a mystery to me, but I have faith in it; light is the creator. If only we had chlorophyll in our veins, could we lie in the sun all day and could changes occur? Could fragments of thought be braided together into strands to create cleverer and more robust ideas? Could a synthesis of all of our loosely tangled memories occur which would leave us nodding and satisfied, like a begonia? Or would our secrets fall from bursting seed pods and be carried away, caught up by the fur of a passing dog, or blown and blown until they are completely taken from us?

I am sure that no one remembers this like I do. Richard was out and Elizabeth had moved back home because Peg was out of the hospital and feeling better. Some neighbours came around one summer evening, must have been in 1968, oh yes, most certainly it was, the last summer Dad was with us. There were three men, Jim Malcolm, Phil Hansen, and Harvey Prefontaine, and one woman, Eva Ferguson, a small parliament of neighbours concerned about Louise and us kids, worried about Duncan. They were dressed in Sunday-type clothing, indicating that to do this thing, to offer advice, had not been undertaken lightly. There may have been a church meeting, or at least several phone calls. No individual would have done such a thing; it was the community's idea we had there in our house.

They talked to Louise in the living room while Dad sat at the kitchen table listening to the radio whine in and out of tune as it often did on summer evenings. When the sky was cloudless, it seemed the signals went amiss. "It's the satellites," Dad used to say. I could not stay in the kitchen with him. It was an act of disloyalty, I knew, but the voices from the living room were so solemn and barely inflected, like those used in the Unity funeral parlour, that I thought most certainly a better situation could be conjured up for us.

I stood in the doorway and was grateful not to be sent away. There was an old chandelier-style light fixture, painted gold and supporting four brilliant light bulbs, all one hundred watts they must have been because the room was garishly lit and the men's white shirts could scarcely be looked at. I listened to the painful talk. Duncan had been doing some odd things, people knew, that summer. Driving in the afternoon, for example, even if it rained, with the windows down and his arm out, fingers hooked along the roof; then, asking Lorne Pope to write his cheque for him at the feed mill, fill in the particulars so that Dad only had to sign. Building bonfires every other night; I was embarrassed to learn that they had found this out. In fact, this had been going on for probably three weeks in the front field. Each night he had cut more branches from the dying elm. I believe he wanted to feel strong sensations on his face, water splashing and fire heating him.

Mrs. Ferguson said, "It must be very hard for you, Louise."

Mom lit a cigarette and said, after thinking, "At times it is, Eva," for which I was grateful. Only at times, she had said.

Jim Malcolm coughed into his hand, then said, "Jack Wallis had problems, you know, like this, every year for a long time and then last year he just didn't come out of it. He sat in his chair for the entire spring and eventually Lois had to drive him to the Regional. She had no choice. It was that or go under."

Mrs. Ferguson went on. "People can say all they want about the Regional, but Jack swears by it. He had those treatments and he's felt better ever since. He says it himself."

I knew this for a fact. He had told even me, an eleven-year-old looking at the *Mad* magazine in the five to a dollar store, after I asked him how he was, just to be polite. "Much better, much better," he had said and then made a zapping sound and laughed, and it had seemed to me that he had been glowing as if filled with electricity, as if sparks might jump out of his ears.

Mom was actually, I think, moved by their concern, knowing how difficult it must have been for them to assemble for this intimate cause. We were all bound together for a moment without shame, thinking of Dad as the one who must run naked out of the burning house. We would simply and wordlessly wrap him in blankets and never mention it again.

Out in the kitchen, the radio had become just a lot of sputtering, frying sounds. I must have wanted to say something to Dad, because I joined him for a moment, circling the table three or four times, not looking at his face or any part of him, but the mainstays of the kitchen – fridge, stove, and the snowy counter light Dad liked to leave on when we watched TV.

The neighbours left and Richard came home, dropped off by other neighbours, so that the yard was festive for a few moments as I watched from my room. There were voices calling and doors slamming and engines turning over. I wonder how it all sounded to Dad. Probably the way our birthday party sounded, I thought, the time I fell sick and had to stay in bed.

I always did have the best bedroom, with that old grate open straight through to the kitchen. I could see the top of Dad's head awaiting judgment or something final because his fingers were drumming on the oilcloth, sticking a bit as he lifted each one. I thought of descending into the kitchen with some new and marvellous sight, an octagonal stamp from Albania, or the telescope trained on the moon in such a way that footprints could be seen. Richard came upstairs to his room and my worry about what Mom would say fell in on me like a sickness suddenly will. There was to be no magic gift to rescue Dad, and so I lay with my cheek resting on the summer-cool, black grate to listen. Through the wall I could hear Richard putting things into his closet.

Mom sat next to Dad and said, "We've been talking about Jack Wallis and the time he spent at the Regional. They helped him out there, Duncan. He's felt better now for several months."

There was no sound. Mom had turned the radio off.

"It's been almost six weeks now you've been like this, Duncan. The kids and I can't do the harvesting and everything else." There was more silence and I realized that Mom was crying, and then there was the match striking and the cigarette smoke winding upward to my grate. I have always associated cigarette smoke with firm resolve and right action. Mom blew her nose and smoked and the fridge hummed and then rattled into rest. I stood up, wanting to hear no more, seeing only Dad's hand on Mom's, far away it seemed, several floors below.

The next morning there was one of those notes, "Paper covers rock." Still, that day, all was well. We knew in the morning that Dad was better; he was talking to Mom and eating fried eggs in his old, good way, and Mom was radiant, a little bit like Jack Wallis had been, skin shining and a red scarf she liked to wear knotted around her neck. All was well, we knew, as Mom turned the radio on to the local channel where coming events could be heard and the marine weather report with the recorded splashing and seagull calls in the background.

I had brought the note downstairs in the pocket of my shorts and it remained with me throughout that still and sunny day. I had no idea what it meant, only that it was a burdensome thing, even with Dad better.

Sitting on the bench beneath the maple tree, I watched Richard and Mom and Dad walk to the shed, their shadows barely grown, too small to lose any part in the maple's shade. I followed later into the cool shed with its vice where we crushed the Quaker State oil cans and the old, wooden trough where, Richard once told me, a pig had been butchered. There was greasing of machinery to be done. Everyone was gathered around the swather so I stood next to Richard as Dad greased and muttered about buying a combine. The swather seemed old and fragile, dinosaur bones in a museum, and I wonder now, looking back, if Dad would not have been happier as a paleontologist digging in the Gobi desert. We could have been the enraptured tribespeople, watching in our robes and scarves, dyed with the petals of flowers, bewildered by what this man was doing.

There were parts to be replaced and some tightening of the canvas to be done. Almost every year a cat would lose a leg to its saw teeth and I worried briefly for them all as the tractor was attached and man and machine rattled forth from the shed, sending a group of sparrows from the rangy Manitoba maple trees.

The field of oats was yellow as the sun could make it, the yellow of civilization and the valleys in Egypt we had learned about in school. Dad circled the field and the oats fell in quick symmetry, and as the afternoon passed we began to feel certain that, indeed, all was well again.

Elizabeth and Mom played charades with us for a while on the front porch. Mom had been reading some political science text and chose as a phrase to pantomime, "the value of labour." She made dollar signs in the air and Elizabeth immediately guessed "money is the root of all evil." I remember Mom frantically digging and hoeing as the three of us watched her, completely befuddled. She stooked sheaves, hammered and ironed clothes. Then, she made a stomach and grimaced as if in pain and Elizabeth shouted "labour." That was as close as we got to the answer.

This morning as I sat in the sun, as the sun did its work, I could see Mom so clearly with her dollar signs and cash register, making motions of payment with a polite expression on her face, between moments of histrionic cajoling and rolling of eyes. And I remembered thinking back then, how funny this game of charades was, to withhold and make others guess. I had realized at that moment, in a childish and concrete way, that when it comes to hiding places, the human mind has no rival. That thought had made Mom's head appear comical, bobbing up and down with its secret and I started laughing, and saying "I give up." We were so relieved to have Mom at last tell us the answer, which made no particular sense to us, and to be able to stop and listen for a while to the sound of the tractor's engine out in the northwest corner of the farm.

Well, there is no such noise here. All of the agriculture on this island seems to involve only people, plants, animals and, of course, the sunlight, which was beginning to swirl in my head like the searchlights of my dream by the time I headed back inside this morning to find Miranda at home finally. It is hot again today, very hot, and close, as if we were all being held in the palm of a large and sweaty hand.

RICHARD

Richard walked across the campus to the bus stop. The late afternoon light had such a white clarity to it that he felt as if he had travelled backward in time, to a period when photographers had not had the option of colour. "I could be the subject of a Lewis Hine photo," he said to himself. "A pale, tired, underpaid and oppressed librarian, walking beneath the trees. 'University library shop steward,' the title would read. And I would be carrying a bag similar to the one I own now, which would be filled with documentation, filled with very brief accounts of unfortunate accidents which had occurred, involving my colleagues, due to inadequate safety standards. Accidents with carts, accidents with shelves. And I would be a good shop steward. Not only would I carry and read those short anecdotes, I would do something to redress the situation. I would sit up late at night, caring."

In actual fact, Richard's briefcase was almost empty except for the articles he had photocopied from fifth floor journals that day, some pieces for Joel from the psychiatric reference materials and, for himself, an abstract of an experiment involving mice breathing underwater. There came a blast of music from MacEwan Hall and Richard began to walk to the beat, contemplating hurling his brief-case into the branches of a spruce tree and breaking into dance, a eurythmic interpretation of the chaos within and around him. He pictured himself growling and pawing at the air, grunting and shouting and pointing sticks at his astonished audience. He would lose himself in a paean to anarchy and dishevelment, and it would be written up in the campus newspaper to be read, in time, by his supervisor Margaret Bain. She would bring Richard's outburst to the attention of the head librarian, Victor Guest. Richard would be asked to resign. This scenario pleased and amused him, although his pleasure was undermined by that oh-so-familiar and yet vague fear that he might be going off the rails.

There was some reassurance to be gained from the fact that he had spoken to Sandra, at last, and Richard believed himself to be a better citizen because of it, even though it was she who had initi-ated the conversation. Sandra had surprised Richard at his fifth floor information desk and he had immediately begun to apologize for avoiding her on past occasions when she had come looking for him, and for not answering the phone.

"I know it's cowardly on my part and I have no real explana-tion for my behaviour other than that I feel a need to be on a kind of, I'm not sure what, a leave of absence, I guess. For a while."

Sandra had stared at him in a way that provoked anxiety and caused Richard to continue talking. "I think it's time to pause and take stock, you know re-evaluate and so on, all those things we're supposed to do nowadays. I need to ask myself where I'm going, examine where I'm coming from, what my time lines are and so on." He knew that this was a wad of bullshit and decided to shut up before Sandra, who knew him well, laughed out loud. Stopping then, and looking at Sandra, for the first time Richard had recog-nized why she often reminded him of an Easter Island sculpture; it was her large forehead and somber expression.

Sandra was not the type to speak out on her heart's behalf. Richard knew this. No doubt, she wanted to ask, "What about us?

What about me?" No doubt she wanted to say, "I know it isn't really a conventional type of relationship with dates and dining and dancing and so on, but it is a relationship, isn't it?"

Instead, Sandra nodded her head a few times and said, "They tell me my cat has feline leukemia."

"I'm sorry to hear that."

"Good. And the record function on my tape-player seems to have died. That's not all, of course, other things have been happening, some good, but I don't wish to discuss them at this time. I'd like you to hear about all of these unfortunate occurrences. Let's see, was there a grease fire in my kitchen? No, I just worried that there might be the night I made french fries. No fires, but I do believe the clutch is going in my car. It was doing very strange things as I drove across the Fourth Street bridge this morning, and speaking of which, bridge, that is, I guess your leave of absence means you won't be playing bridge with us on Thursday night."

"Yes, I guess that's true," Richard answered flatly, and Sandra's posture had the look of someone absorbing a weight, as if Richard had heaved a very large phone book to her.

"Well, call me when you get back home," Sandra said, finding a pen on his desk and printing "ASSHOLE" in capital letters across a blank piece of paper. But by the time Sandra had disappeared down the stairwell, Richard was admitting to himself that a situation defined always brought him relief. And he felt that the situation was now defined.

Other situations remained undefined, however, and as he waited for the bus Richard began to recall the events of the previous evening with Joel and Nora. They had come to his place for a beer, although Nora had decided that she would rather have vodka, and Richard had observed a louder quality to Nora, a proclamation in her behaviour that suggested intimacy with Joel. Listening to reggae music, for example, she suddenly suggested that they all do the limbo. "It seems that athletic stunts are associated with drinking for Nora," Joel had said fondly.

Nora had been able to limbo the lowest, and then Joel had touched her hair as they sat on the couch, and Nora had licked potato chip crumbs from her fingers in an exaggerated way, Richard had thought, as if to provide an illustrative example of the act of licking.

Perhaps it's all in my imagination, Richard thought. Perhaps I exaggerate and there is nothing going on between those two, and Joel was not touching Nora's hair but actually picking dog hair from the couch. Most likely. And he became tired all of a sudden and realized he was running out of steam, and he asked himself what it really mattered, in that recumbent afternoon light. Soon he would be home and, this being Friday, once there, he would prepare himself a vodka martini.

In his mailbox when he arrived was a small package from Gayle containing photographs and a letter that read, "Here are some pictures of the people here: Charlie, Pui Sin, Elizabeth, Miranda and me. One of each. We were all at Charlie and Pui Sin's house at the time. I like the cigarette smoke in Pui Sin's picture. Everything just hangs these days. Nothing blows. Take a close look at Miranda and tell me what you think. It is so beautiful here, and other-worldly, old-worldly. I feel in the power of something else, like the plastic bags on the water I watch each time I am at the beach. I am pulled a little toward home, but the undercurrent sweeps me back. Remember how terrified we always used to be of the undertow on stormy days? We'd stand on the beach and watch the waves and talk and marvel at what was being dragged away beneath the surface. About how fast it could suck you under, just like quicksand, until Iris Chesney came along and chased us away, of course. Being sucked under and pulled away and blown upwards were a few of the favourite topics of childhood. It seems that we were more open to the big influences, back then. I think of you all the time. Love, Gayle."

Richard had not thought about Iris Chesney for a long time. Iris's cottage, which was her year-round home, sat right on the beach, not far from the base of the cat-walk. For many years she had kept an eye on Richard and Gayle, convinced as she was that "some disturbance might exist." Richard knew that even in recent years, back in Unity, Iris had been overheard commenting that, "Frankly, she was surprised that Richard and Gayle McDonagh had turned out as well as they had."

Iris had never trusted Gayle and Richard down by the water, and seemed for years to think them capable of only the most irrational of acts. The summer when Gayle and Richard were eight years old, they had been busying themselves one afternoon on the beach mixing sand and water and spiny beach grass into a discarded ginger ale bottle, when Iris strolled up to them and said,

"You won't go drinking that now, will you?" Gayle had looked at Iris as if she had said, "You won't go strangling your dog now, will you?" They learned to play with their backs to Iris's living room window, but accepted that nothing would stop the inevitable intrusions of Iris, wearing her mannish cardigan and the baggy trousers Gayle later began to refer to as "Iris's palazzo pants."

Iris knew things that others did not. She had read extensively the work of Freud and Jung, and had cards printed bearing her name and the title "Student of Human Nature." She liked to use phrases such as "oedipal complex" or "animus" and believed firmly that Duncan McDonagh needed to see a psychiatrist.

Iris's clinical interests were, mercifully, tempered by her envy and admiration of achievement in others. She wrote a column for the *Unity Informer* titled "Personals with a Difference," in which she made clear her disdain for the conventional personal columns in neighbouring weeklies, with their attention to family outings and junkets to Owen Sound. Those members of the community considered important and informed were called regularly for their opinions on current affairs, and these were printed in editorial fashion. Louise McDonagh was called often and it was an ongoing, anticipated irritation to Iris that, when she called, Louise was rarely home, but Duncan was.

Iris did not wish to speak with Duncan. Duncan, on the other hand, if caught in a good frame of mind, delighted in talking to Iris. He held her in high esteem, and Richard guessed now that this was possibly because of her central position in the communication of ideas in Unity. Duncan may have seen Iris as one of the filaments from his ideal circumstance.

When Iris called, Duncan would offer his thoughts and musings, often dictating in the third person. "Duncan McDonagh enjoyed his last swim of the season today," he would say. "Braving the whitecaps and unseasonably low autumnal temperatures, he took to the water while a handful of onlookers applauded from Keat's dock. 'You looked like a raisin in the sun out there,' his daughter, Gayle, observed at the conclusion of the swim." Or, at another time, Duncan might say, "Iris, I want you to ask your readership, 'Is this really adequate?' I know you do your best to print the issues and achievements of the week, and I applaud you for that, but what I want to know is, does your column tell the true story or are there adventures going on we don't know about? Are the Formans, for example, harbouring illegal immigrants in their root cellar, who swarm forth at night to pick earthworms from the soil? And what about that crater that appeared in the Radkes' field? Where did it come from anyway? And the tunnels they say exist from the old jail down to where the nuclear power plant is now, what's the connection there?"

Duncan always grinned as he talked to Iris. He knew that none of his thoughts would ever be published. As soon as she possibly could, Iris would ask when Louise was expected back, claiming to be "pressed. You know how it is in the newspaper business, deadlines, deadlines."

Richard thought about the box of old *Informers* in his closet. He had begun collecting them early on in 1967, centennial year, when his mother had been involved in the centennial project, "The Energy Speakers Series." A *Toronto Star* reporter had come to Unity to do an article on their project; it was the juxtaposition of the nuclear power plant on the lakeshore and the speakers' topics that had caught her interest. And when Iris (the *Informer*'s photographer as well) took a picture of the *Star* reporter with Louise, Richard and Gayle tacking up one of their "Nuclear Threat" posters, Richard's collection had begun. It was discontinued when the reports on his father's disappearance began. Only the first account, with the headlines, had been kept, along with all the other weeklies, in Richard's square Hiram and Walker's box. He thought of looking through them, scanning issue after issue for the Brieflies he knew had been titled "Snapshots," but decided against it.

Drinking his martini very slowly and sitting upon his wheeled chair, Richard was aware of a certain loneliness having caught up with him, and he reached for the envelope containing Gayle's photographs. As he glanced through them, his first thought was that they were in no way like the hypothetical Lewis Hine shot of himself leaving work, with his hunched back and his briefcase. Why do they all look so content, Richard wondered, and why is the background so gauzy in appearance? Did they hang a scrim before taking these? Placing all of the pictures upon his kitchen table, Richard admitted to feeling jealous of their sub-tropical complexions and the sub-tropical candour with which they all had looked into the camera lens.

There was Pui Sin with the white eye and the cigarette between first and second finger, and the aforementioned smoke which wavered in bands like little ribs, cat ribs maybe, above her hand. Charlie was laughing. He was large and knowing and vigorous in appearance, Richard thought, having that look of men who have seen war and devastation and the scraping away of life, and now attend to details such as the igniting of fireworks at a New Year's party. Elizabeth leaned forward in her chair and Richard knew from this that she had been interrupted in conversation to have this portrait taken. And this must be Miranda, Richard thought, admiring the photograph of a pale woman holding a bone coloured cup to her lips. She was wearing the melancholy black-fringed hat, and her face was partially in shade, but the eyes were visible and direct.

Gayle was biting into a tomato and seeds and reddish juice were exploding outward, like the happiness which was obvious on her face. She was happy with Miranda's presence, Richard could tell from thousands of miles away. She was blushing with the pleasure of biting into the windless evening. She would have bitten into Miranda's heart right then and there, Richard thought, sending its seeds sailing out, leaving them to stick like small bits of meat upon book covers and teacups and anything else nearby.

Richard imagined their sounds that night rising around them like a scent, private and close-in. He recognized his loneliness again and wondered if it felt the same for everyone, or if some felt it like a fear, and others like a sudden weakening in the knees or a deadening of the skin. For Richard, it was a disquieting lack of anticipation, like watching the dryers spin at the laundromat, or getting into bed and realizing he was not tired after all.

He felt a little foolish then about what he wanted to do, but went ahead and took the shoebox of photographs from his bookshelf. Finding a picture of himself, he nudged it between Gayle and Elizabeth on the table, and felt better. "There," he said, "I am uplifted." And he sat up straight and thought, "Even my posture improves and I begin to consider washing the two days' worth of dishes in the sink. Or perhaps I should move onward to the sweeping up of the bits of shredded wheat on this kitchen floor. Yes, a person must go onward, Iris would agree, onward to the next moment's fallibility," and Richard began to search for the broom which had been misplaced by Nora after the limbo session of the night before.

Gayle

Oh my. I awoke with my right arm paralyzed from sleeping with it under my head. So detached did this limb seem to me that my first thought was that it belonged to Joel and I looked for him, automatically, before I began moving the fingers with my left hand and the tingling life returned. Joel's usual response to any form of sleep paralysis is to wake me and tell me that he thinks he has had a stroke. And, even though he will laugh at himself, he will still go to the bathroom to check his facial muscles. Joel knows the names of all of the cranial nerves and where they operate.

I had decided to call Joel last night and perhaps that is why he was on my mind. I wanted to talk to him about that "paper covers rock" note; I felt that I had had an insight. From over here, everything can look different, even a twenty-year-old note. And so, this morning, after a few moments of guilt and pathos at the remembrance of

Joel's hypochondriasis, I called him.

He answered on the third ring. For some reason, the distance I suppose, I was prepared for a longer wait, maybe a dozen rings. We began by talking about sweat and the fact that we both have been sweating day and night, with very little in the way of sleep. There was a silence which I must admit seemed just as wide, if not wider, than the ocean. So I leaped right into the subject at hand, telling Joel that I had been thinking about that note of Duncan's and that I had come to the conclusion that it meant that Dad had made a decision. I said that I had thought in the past that it meant that he had decided to get a grip on himself and get back on track, but that I had changed my mind. I said that I now thought that he had decided that night that he would leave and that by the time he actually did go, he had had a destination in mind. It had not been just a departure from us, he had not just sunk himself in Lake Huron.

There was no response from Joel; I imagined submarines gliding over trans-oceanic cables.

"You mean you think," Joel finally said, "that your father spent that summer and fall making detailed plans to go somewhere and begin another life. You arrived at this conclusion on the basis of the 'paper covers rock' note?"

"Yes," I said.

"How?"

"I don't think a person would allude to paper covering rock unless he were referring to a carefully thought out procedure. You know, paper, rock, scissors. It's a game, but it's a method of decision-making."

"And the outcome is random," Joel added.

There was another silence after that observation. It undid me, I must admit. You know how it is possible to experience belief or understanding or insight, but only for the briefest moment in time? It is like listening to rumours, weak and pleasing little rumours, interior gossipings which we wish borne out, but which are so insubstantial that with only a breath of dispute they are abandoned. That is how it was with Joel, and I agreed, "Yes, the outcome is random."

He asked, "When are you coming back?"

And I said, "Soon, very soon. August. No later than Labour Day."

And then, "I miss you." But both claims felt very much like lies. Not much more was said. I said "good-bye" and Joel answered with "Yeah, right" and hung up, after which I paced the hall for a while and banged my head, just once, on the wall, leaving a small indentation only I will ever notice.

It is not entirely a lie to say that I miss Joel, but it is a pretence to state that I am making plans to return, because I am not. I have been here hardly any time at all, not even one season, and the months before me on the calendar have the look and feel of an itinerary with numbers denoting very significant motion to be undertaken, speeds, distances to be travelled, places to be drawn closer to. Why leave a sub-tropical zone for a temperate zone just yet? And I haven't said a word to Elizabeth yet about Dad. I keep hoping some inspiration will come to me, simply from being near her. But the "paper covers rock" one was not much help.

Elizabeth had been in the shower while I talked with Joel and when she came out of the bathroom and crouched in front of our dwarf refrigerator, shaking a carton of milk, I had to say something. I was perturbed. I had a feeling of wanting to throw something playfully, like a frisbee, only a bit too hard, a bit too fast, a little aggressively, with my teeth showing.

"That's not really necessary you know, shaking that milk," I said. "It's been homogenized. You know that homogenized milk doesn't need to be shaken. You should know that, you grew up on a farm. You know that the fat globules have already been broken up and distributed evenly throughout the milk. You're wasting your wrist muscles doing that. It's only the milk Miranda gets from the monastery that needs to be shaken because it's not homogenized."

By the time I had arrived at the third pronunciation of the word "homogenized," I was inflamed with a desire to prove a point, any point at all, in a controlled and irrefutable manner, as if delivering a prepared speech at the Toastmistress Club. I wished that I knew more about the subtle influences of chemistry upon our daily lives.

As Elizabeth looked upward with raised eyebrows, I said, "I've noticed you doing that before, shaking the cartons like that." And that was my final summation before closing the bathroom door behind me.

The toilet paper was again wet from those who had showered before me, so I entered Jocelyn's private bag. There were a couple of new items which caught my interest, a series of four pictures of her father and her, taken in one of those instant photo booths, and a note her mother had written saying, "Dear Joc, I will be very late tonight. Here is some money for fish soup. I love you. Mommy."

By the time I finished showering, Elizabeth had gone out. I wanted to be on the ferry soon, so I dressed quickly, leaving ten dollars H.K. in the blue cup with the lid which has become a mail box for Jocelyn and me since her mother began working again, this time for a travel agency. Jocelyn would find the money there and buy fried rice and popsicles for Willy and herself. Then I took off running, with wet hair, to the dock. I realized that I had not run anywhere since the heat arrived and I had the faulty impression that I could outdistance it or break through a meteorological barrier into a place where the plants are spiny or sapless, unearthed, scattered by the wind; none of these thick-leaved, succulent and panting things.

Economy class on the ferry is wide open, no window-panes, unlike the strangely floating first class with its glassed in flat air, hung with the odour of instant coffee and San Miguel beer. I always choose economy. This morning I had an assignment from Charlie. He had learned of a fire at a Leningrad library and wanted me to look through the newspapers at the university for any reference to it, no matter how insignificant. After that, I was to meet Miranda for lunch. She had asked me and I was very excited by that. I wondered what it meant, if it meant anything at all, and that is all I really thought about for the hour long ferry ride. In an untroubled, meditative way, I breathed in the ocean and watched the mothers dangle their toddlers over the railing to pee into the water.

Soon enough the ferry crashed into the great tires along the dock and everyone lurched like commuters on a train, in the same expressionless way, then scurried onto land and into the fumes and haste. Despite all of the news about the economic changes to come here, there still seems to be plenty of money flying around. But I was standing on the nether side of the world of finance, waiting for the double decker bus to carry me up the hill to the tables and fans of the library.

The newspapers are kept in drawers. Charlie had said that as far as he knew it had happened in April, so I began with the *New York Times*, April first edition. I luxuriated in my work, daydreaming and watching the students, wondering if any were studying botany, taking notes for a mid-term paper on the topic of seed dormancy. I began to think about seeds and fertility and my own two nests of eggs, every month supplying an autonomous half-self to swim off in search of a partner. Is there a cumulative frustration for them as the years pass? Do they tear themselves from the parent organ with greater ferocity, and then wait, wait, wait among the draperies of the fallopian tubes? Joel wants children, he wants a family. I think I would be a terrible mother. He probably thinks that too, now.

Miranda has had an abortion. She told me recently in the manner that she will, as we were in the market admiring the red bananas. "It was thirteen years ago today that I had an abortion. I always commemorate it in some way, some inner way," she said. "It's another life now I suppose, so I choose something to honour, or possibly respect, for the day, even if it is only the ingredients for a soup. I pay more attention on this day."

I did not ask any questions, why, with whom, or what about the Catholicism, although observing the style in which she tends to Willy and Jocelyn, it was probably for the best.

What I considered instead were the cannula and suction, the instruments inside her most vulnerable flesh, and wondered if the doctor and nurse had been kind, if they had patted her forehead or if they had been busy with their own conversation above her, words sailing through the air, banging into Miranda's skull with that boneless sound June bugs can produce. She would have been afraid. And, I thought, I most likely would have been at home in Unity, waiting to go off to university, contentedly observing the sea of Icelandic and opium poppies that had taken over the yard behind the house in their fecund, pastel manner. I often imagine these parallel types of scenes when listening to Miranda.

As I searched the papers, I became more and more happy about meeting Miranda for lunch. I imagined her at the travel agency in her secretarial clothes, nylons and the shoes she never wears at home. Some people, in working costume, appear so tentative, so prepared to flee; that is Miranda. It was provocative to imagine her typing or standing distractedly at the copying machine.

We are at least more intimate than the world of business affairs would allow, I assured myself.

Charlie's reference was located without much trouble, in the *Manchester Guardian*, and I began to write. "Major fire at Leningrad library. Book lovers from around the world are converging in Leningrad to try to alleviate what some say is the literary equivalent of Chernobyl – a fire which destroyed or damaged millions of books and was initially covered up." In fact, the fire had occurred in February; I would say this to Charlie, I planned, when I returned in the afternoon. "Like a death in the family for bibliophiles," I would say with pomposity, before he had had an opportunity to read what I had written.

It was luck to have located the reference so quickly. I took the bus back down the hill and walked to Wing On Street, becoming almost somnambulant, so vigorous and tiring was my anticipation. I felt as if I were just a bit of roving colour, like the bolts of fabric being moved here and there by the vendors. "Special fall colour," one man said, "special summer price." I moved past the yellows and blues to the rust piece of silk the merchant was holding. Touching it, I was reminded of the rounded bits of red brick that are thrown onto the beaches of Lake Huron.

"Yes, I'll have some," I said. "Four yards, please." The cloth was cut and placed inside an orange plastic bag.

There was time to go to the China Department Store and buy Charlie his fish emulsion and the toothpaste he likes. Behind the counter were jars filled with what appeared to be mossy antlers, poplar roots and yellow spores collected from mushrooms. I wanted to order up something aphrodisiacal, a leavening agent, a quickening potion, a rare enzyme that could cause hearts to cleave together. Instead, I paid for Charlie's supplies and then had two plastic bags.

There were jade bracelets on the sidewalk, which I touched, before a side trip to a stone wall and a fig tree I have visited before. It is possible to watch the Star Ferry from there, chugging back and forth between the mainland and the island. At night it is especially beautiful, the water reflecting so many lights it is as if some movable embroidery had been worked. I waited there for a few minutes, giving Miranda a chance to arrive at the restaurant before me, wanting her to be able to watch me enter.

No such luck. Miranda was nowhere to be seen in the restaurant when I arrived. Tea was brought and I said, "I'm waiting for a friend," then took out, one by one, the items I had bought for Charlie, and the silk, admiring them as shoppers invariably will do, preparing what I might say to Miranda and wondering if I could be the amusing one this time. I read and re-read the newspaper piece. I memorized it. It was something to bring along as I waded out into my dejection, without a word of anything to myself, mind you. An hour had passed before I allowed the thought, "Miranda has forgotten," and ordered lunch for myself.

To have been the event forgotten requires some homage to the self, so I bought roses for myself and took them home, but of course when Miranda arrived, wanted to give them to her. I resisted that impulse, however. Leaving them on the table in the hallway, and standing so that I could touch them with my left hand if I had wanted to, I said to Miranda, "I missed you at lunch today."

She was drying Willy's hair with a towel, which she then held to her mouth, speaking muffled but genuine apologies about having completely forgotten. "That's okay," I said. What else could I have said? "The food was great. We can do it some other time."

"I promise I won't forget," she said, and the evening became at once very pleasant. At least Maurice has not been here for several days and Miranda has been home in the evenings. Out on the balcony, I sat and read beneath the fluorescent light. The Chinese flag, belonging to the communists next door, blew on to the railing and fell away.

Jocelyn brought me a picture from the dentist's clinic she had coloured. It read, "Plaque, the bug that eats teeth." The plaque bug was a brown and green crab-like cell with tridents in its several arms and beneath, written in pencil, was the following instruction from Jocelyn. "Please keep forever in a safe, dry place."

I thanked her and folded the picture and placed it inside my book, thinking for a while about the preservation of things and how difficult it is, especially here in this wet and humid place. And then I thought that there are times when it is unfortunate that memories never spoil, there is no specified shelf life for them, no expiration date after which they might as well be tossed away. It must be safe and dry inside the mind, because the distant memories are really no more or less worm-eaten than the recent ones it seems.

Richard

Richard was sitting in robe and slippers, reading a brief account of a van filled with Canadians which had been washed away in a mud slide in Quito. They had been architecture students from Vancouver, taking photographs of Ecuadoran structures. Possibly one had needed to stop for cigarettes, Richard speculated, somewhere along the way, causing the van and the mud's unfortunate timing. Or, maybe the mud had begun to detach itself at the very moment their plane arrived, two weeks earlier, and had been swelling ever since so that the rumbling of the van's tires was all that was needed.

No, it had to have been more epic, Richard thought. For decades, since the mid-sixties when all of these students were born, deposits of sandy soil had been building, over the years, through day after day of newspaper headlines about the space shuttle and the Falkland Islands and Halley's Comet. It had been accumulating as the students lived their daily lives on another continent and in an ease that would never have suspected mud slides as a fate. And yet, there must have been some lineage somewhere, a cousin or a step-mother living outside of Quito who had written saying, "Come to Ecuador, come to Quito, this is the best road to take."

Unlikely, Richard had to admit. It was the fault of the one who had stopped for cigarettes. Five minutes earlier or later, that is all it would have taken; that's the way of life. And then, off they all went, unknowing, unknowing, a truckload of intimates by that time, a moving community hall with the habits and diseases of everyone fully public. That was what disturbed Richard most, that this interior place of thinking and planning could have been swept away by so much unintentioned mud.

He clipped this piece from the paper and began skimming a few articles photocopied from journals of physics, history and medicine. All information related to medicine was handed over to Joel. The physics and history were Richard's. There was also an article from *The Atlantic* on the possibility of communicating with life elsewhere in the galaxy.

Daily Richard located more and more information which seemed to him to be not only vital, but also connected, kindred, as if he were constructing a genealogy of facts. Each find sent him skittering to the photocopy machine, thinking to himself, "This is madness," especially now that his supervisor, Margaret Bain, had begun watching him from her office door.

She had questioned him on Thursday, saying, "Richard, I must say that I am a bit nonplussed by the amount of photocopying you have been doing. You know everyone is very serious about the new copyright law." Margaret's use of the word "nonplussed" invariably denoted vexation.

She was a tall woman, practically as tall as Richard, and her eyes had been very grey as they looked into his. Richard had thought to himself, "These are the eyes of the letter of the law, the eyes that read the finest of print," and, experiencing a cerebral little guffaw, he had said to Margaret, "I'm developing some new handouts for the student tours, slightly more pragmatic than the old ones, I think. My aim is to make the tour more of a hands-on type of experience." Hands-on was a favourite term of Margaret's.

"I shall be very interested in seeing your work," had been Margaret's terse reply.

"I'm rather excited about it myself," Richard had said, knowing that the tautness of Margaret's skirt, with each stride as she walked away, spoke of inner seething. Yet, he had not cared.

On this Saturday morning, though, before the day had tranquilized itself into afternoon, Richard took time to worry about his indifference in the face of Margaret's disapproval. It was not like him. Normally, he would have been more concerned; he knew he would have behaved in exactly the same manner, but still have been shaken up. He would have begun immediately to look for a pink slip in his pay envelope, or thought about, but never acted upon, an apology or some means of reconciling with Margaret. His indifference had surprised him even as Margaret spoke, and it had remained with him throughout the remainder of Thursday and Friday, a sort of lens through which to look back at Margaret as she watched him. This freedom from concern about Margaret made Richard's morning queer and exciting, the way a shocking news report—heard first thing from the alarm radio—will. Yes, it was exciting and queer that he did not care and, furthermore, was not worried that he had no intention to begin to care. "I have become a bold insouciant," Richard said to himself as he made plans to photocopy more, and brazenly, on Monday.

Richard turned back to his reading. There were three steps to this activity—skimming, underlining and filing by category. Richard never read research articles in their entirety. In his opinion they were too long and most often filled with methodologies irrelevant to what he wanted, which was the outcome, the results. In fact, what held his attention best were descriptions of conditions, or syndromes, or events with no clearly understood cause. Richard had collected information on a thyroid condition, for example, Hashimoto's disease, which he read with an intensity of interest. "A type of cannibalism of the immune system," he liked to read over and over again. "No one really understands why the human organism would suddenly begin an assault on one of its own organs."

Richard slipped off his robe and sat in his boxer shorts. The weather had turned hot, too hot, so hot that even though it was still morning he decided that a walk with Reba to Joel's house to deliver the thyroid articles would be a good reason to escape his attic furnace of a home. Joel was now Richard's only social contact and he was thinking, for no good reason whatsoever, that even this should be discontinued for a while.

Reba panted and slobbered as they walked. In keeping with the torpor of the day, after three rings of Joel's bell there was still no answer, so Richard let himself in to the cool hallway.

Nora was there, Richard knew, before she had spoken, before the soft baby dog-talk came from the bedroom where Reba had dashed, past an emerging Joel, in search of Gayle. There were plenty of signs: Nora's sandals and her boy's green jacket with dome fasteners, the type Richard used to wear to the barn. On the kitchen counter could be seen her coffee bean grinder and plunger coffee maker. But these were not nearly as tangible as her presence, which caused Richard to feel as if he were in a gallery or some over-stuffed place of display. "Like the Museum of Science and Industry in Chicago," he said to himself. There was something about Nora that took him back in time, to a less sophisticated era when people could be spellbound in a very warm room by the sight of a giant-sized washing machine agitating a giant family's clothing within a clear plastic drum. Perhaps because Richard feared that would be his reaction, open-mouthed, gaping, when finally forced to realize that Nora was occupying a space in Joel and Gayle's bed.

"Hello, Richard," Nora called from the bedroom. "Come and talk to me. I want to talk to you."

Richard wondered if Nora always felt as he did when conducting student tours in the library, that is, more aroused than others, smarter, in control. He entered the bedroom, wanting to squint his eyes, wanting to move them rapidly around in circles so as to blur the image of Nora in Gayle's bed, but he could not. There she was, reclining, with the blankets tucked in her armpits. Reba had retreated to the kitchen to join Joel in the coffee-making.

"Well, here he is," Nora said. "Here he is."

"Yes, here I am," Richard answered, resting his gaze upon Nora at last, conscious of keeping his mouth closed, his eyes a bit disinterested.

"So," Nora went on. "You're looking well."

It seemed to Richard that Nora was smiling in the way a person will when she has something much better to say, something far more personal to discuss.

"Joel has been telling me about your family," she began.

"Oh no," Richard thought, a quiet and civil complaint, but it seemed to resonate in his own ears like a shout.

"I hope you don't mind me asking, but I'm really very curious. I'm a curious person by nature."

An image of Iris Chesney flashed through Richard's mind, as he wondered if curious persons by nature were in any way akin to students of human nature.

"Your father," Nora said, "I'd like to hear a bit about him. You never heard from him again after he disappeared?" She paused, and then added, "If you'd rather not talk about it, just say so."

"Oh no, I'm not bothered by talking about it," Richard said, lying deliberately and wondering why he seemed to want to misrepresent himself to Nora. "I feel quite at ease here, actually," he said, sitting down. "Maybe because this desk chair of Joel's has wheels and I can roll around on it, just as if I were at home."

Joel returned and sat down on the bed, in his T-shirt and underwear. He rotated his left ankle until the joint snapped loudly, like a twig breaking. "Aaaah," he sighed.

"Get under the blankets," Nora said, "Richard's going to tell us a story."

"But Joel's heard it all before, and it's not really a story because I'm not sure where the beginning and ending points are," Richard said.

"Just start," Nora said. "And don't worry about Joel. I'll listen."

"Well, lately I've been thinking it began with the fact that Duncan and Louise married so late, they were in their forties when we were born, you know. This was never made clear, but I think in a way their marriage was a project of the community. Here we had these two eligible and attractive people, Duncan hacking away at the farm, getting nowhere, and Louise, a nurse for fifteen years and ready for a change. There were no romantic tales of how they met because they had known each other all their lives. All of a sudden they were married, and Mom left the hospital and got pregnant and we were born in 1955. I imagine it created quite a stir, Mom having twins at age forty-two. It all seemed normal enough to me and Gayle though."

Nora was looking at Richard with a funny little smile, but he went on. "I've tried to pinpoint when it was Dad first started to be a little strange, and I honestly can't say. He gradually went from being funny in ways we kind of liked, to funny in ways we kind of didn't like. Like when we were little, six or seven, in the fall, he would keep us out of school and spend entire days on the beach with us. He was never big on work. Or he would get us to help him rig up speakers in the chicken coop so the chickens could have music. We thought he was great, and in some ways, at first, Mom did too.

"By 1967, though, there was no denying he was getting a bit weird. So much went on that year, and the next. Aunt Peg, Dad's younger sister, got sick and got better. Elizabeth came and went. Dad was leaving those notes for Gayle and going to church wearing a string tie. He got into a habit of phoning the minister on Saturday night and requesting certain hymns, 'Unto the hills, around do I lift up, my longing eyes,' was a favourite. When we went to school in the mornings we left Dad at the table with his breakfast uneaten and Mom at the counter, mad, reading the paper. Sometimes he would do the milking in the morning, but I think most times Mom did it.

"We didn't hear what went on, really. In the evenings that fall of '68 it was Gayle who got him to the barn. Mom was taking courses through continuing education again, at the high school, so we were often alone with Dad in the evening. Gayle and I took to spending a lot of time in the basement, it was so gloomy upstairs. Dad would sit and listen to the radio on no particular channel which in and of itself could drive a person crazy. It was a cold fall and we had the furnace going. It was a wood-burning furnace which was pretty satisfying to us kids in a lot of ways. You could destroy all sorts of evidence or just look in and imagine what it would be like to be burned alive. Gayle got a note that October that was disturbing. 'I wonder if this longing will end,' it read. She burned it – let me read it first, then threw it in and we never talked about it again. When Mom was home, we weren't allowed to sit down there. To her, any kind of withdrawal was an unhealthy sign.

"November was just bleak, as far as I can recall, thirty days of bleakness. I don't remember Dad saying a word, although I am sure he must have. Mom worried more and more about bills and money, and she and Peg tried to get him to go to the doctor, which I guess he did do, but, once he was there, he talked a good line so the doctor never thought there was anything wrong with him. I remember Gayle saying during that time that she thought Dad was turning invisible, losing his ability to reflect light. She didn't think she could see him properly."

Nora put an arm around Joel, but her eyes were fixed on Richard. Her attention pleased him.

"Anyway, on the afternoon of December fourth we came home from school and Mom and Dad were having a drink together, rye and ginger ale probably, and they were laughing. Dad was walking around with his thick wool socks on and a white shirt, very bright again, and his black hair was the way it normally was, that is, clean and brushed back from his forehead, and Mom was wearing the dress she had bought for the election. Her cheeks and ears were pink. Dad was better again.

"He was happy to see us and said, 'Let's call Elizabeth and see if she wants to come over and work on the stamp album after chores.' Gayle wanted to walk over though, not phone—it wasn't far—which is what we did, right after supper. Our first instinct when Dad was better was to get out of his sight, as if the way we handled him might cause some damage. He was like the plaster of paris ornaments we made in elementary school which were never totally set, always dropping a limb or a head just when it appeared to be perfect. So, we walked over to Aunt Peg and Uncle Ken's, and there was Elizabeth standing outside beneath the maple tree in her blue beret, watching for her father to come home in his truck. Of course, she wanted to come over. 'It seems as if we've been stuck at Madagascar for so long,' she said, or something like that."

Joel interrupted, saying, "Just a minute," and headed out to the kitchen to pour the boiling water into the coffee pot. Reba came into the bedroom, looked, went out again, still looking, while Nora and Richard sat in silence. Joel returned.

"So, that night, after the chores we all sat down at the kitchen table, except Mom who went to bed early. I think she felt the need to stay clear of Duncan right after one of his changes, too. We were looking for stamps from Martinique; we were all pretty happy. Gayle had a fish in a bucket by the sink. She had found it flopping on the beach a couple of days before and thought it needed rescuing from the winter. Gayle was standing at the counter steaming the backs off of stamps, using the electric kettle and checking on her fish. It was a trout, I think.

"And that turned out to be his last night with us. We didn't know it then, of course. But something that Dad did do that was odd was—he kissed Gayle—good-bye, I guess—while she was standing at the metal bucket with the steam bubbling up behind her. He was standing there too, and all of a sudden he just leaned down and kissed her on the cheek for what seemed to be the longest time, but now that I think of it, it was probably fewer seconds than it takes to speak the average sentence. I mean, it was a chaste kiss, but stretched a little, and with the kettle going it had a drama to it. Elizabeth and I both stared. She had a fairly new camera and had brought it over that night to take some pictures; in fact, she had just taken one before the kiss happened. At any rate, he left that night, or morning, leaving one last note, 'Your father regrets.' I still have that one. Gayle gave them all to me."

"What happened after the kiss that night?" Nora asked.

"Nothing. We carried on with the stamps until about eleven o'clock, news time. It was surprising to us, what he had done, but not really shocking. Maybe we had become immune to shock. Nothing was said of it. Gayle and I went to bed and Elizabeth stayed for a while then walked home, I guess. She was in grade twelve then and studying two different types of math, Math A and Math B, and I remember Dad used to like to get her talking about them, these maths. I'm pretty sure she tried to explain the difference to us that night. These things stick in your mind you know, like what you were doing when you first saw the space shuttle exploding.

"In the morning there was the note, but we didn't know that he was gone. We thought he was in the barn. Maybe he was and he left in the afternoon. Mom said she thought he was cleaning calf pens. She said that to everyone, the police, Iris Chesney, the insurance people who never gave her any money. I'll bet that by afternoon she knew, though. When he didn't show for lunch, she knew." As Richard said this he was aware that he was sounding like the many friends and relatives and neighbours who had mulled over Duncan's disappearance, and Louise's reaction, and talked and speculated and talked and speculated. To recall this made him tired. Richard wanted to stop talking, wanted to wrap things up but wasn't sure how to go about it.

"Gayle kept the note in her pencil case for months, and wore Dad's shirts to school. It was a bad time." Looking at Joel and Nora, he repeated, "It was a bad time. Mom and I both accepted more or less that he drowned himself. I've never been sure what Gayle thinks became of him. And I guess that is the end of the story." Richard unfastened his watch band for no reason, then fastened it again.

There was a silence then, not the normal early afternoon silence which occurs between the tickings of the clock, but a heavier, pushing kind, the silence experienced after lawn mowers or power saws are shut off and the listener is very conscious of his ears. They are pricked. Even the vision at such times becomes more acute. Richard realized, with dismay, as he looked at Nora and Joel, that they had begun to look very definitely, very unambiguously coupled, it seemed, and for the briefest of moments he wanted to produce a barking noise, a dog-shout of protest, but naturally he did not. Instead, he called to Reba who dutifully came, carrying her bounty of devotion with her.

Joel rose to pour the coffee, while Nora made far-off mothering kinds of comments, aimed at Richard, which were not heard. He had become preoccupied with a plan to spend even more time alone, not see Joel and Nora for a while. And once that commitment had been made, Richard spoke up brightly about something or other, all the while longing for his stacks and piles, the walled-in mess of his apartment.

GAYLE

I decided today that Elizabeth is the most alert person I know. I tried to think of others who might compare, but came up with no one. When she was a baby, I imagine people commented upon her alertness, just as they will when she is ninety-five and still correcting papers and travelling here and there. "How about that Elizabeth March?" they will ask, with an indulgent smile. Most mornings I emerge from my room wanting to duck my head and run to the bathroom, so as to hide from her alert salvos.

This morning, though, she came into my room to admire my row of stamps. There are eight now and the most recent bears an image of a generic town hall. Elizabeth studied it closely, then began reciting the counties and county towns of Ontario and recalling Miss Peirce, our old teacher, and her fanaticism for details such as Hastings-Belleville, Northumberland-Cobourg. "They're sedating, actually," Elizabeth said, "like a skipping rhyme," although I do not recall Richard or me being particularly calmed by this naming of counties and their principal towns.

I told Elizabeth that Miss Peirce often mentioned what a clever class our cousin had been in. "Four years later," I said, "when we had her as our teacher, she was still saying, 'I've never had a group quite like the one your cousin was in.' With us she couldn't even play her bird call recordings during math because we were too distractible. Those were the days when, if someone had given an especially incorrect answer, Miss Peirce would turn out all the lights as her way of letting us know how dim we all were."

It was because of those counties and county seats that we went off on a hike today, though, so I suppose there is some benefit to Elizabeth's capacity for remembering. She decided that it would be a good idea to go for a long walk and quiz Charlie, allow him to free associate to all of those names like Lennox and Addington. And, because it was Sunday, Miranda and the kids came along.

It was an outing, and an occasion to bring my camera with its new strap. Miranda wove it and presented it to me last Wednesday, for being "so good with the kids" and I have been needlessly happy with it ever since. It is in her signature colours of black and white, but the running figures seem to be wearing turbans this time.

When Charlie saw it, he said, "I see you've officially joined the League of Fools, at last. I knew it would only be a matter of time. Half this island owns a camera strap for goods or services rendered, some chicken wings or a ride to Pui O or a prescription. It's a kind of badge. And then there are the rest of us who possess the dreaded drawings. You've seen mine, haven't you?"

I had not.

"All a jumble of different alphabets and numbers and musical allusions, morse code dots and dashes and even tiny flags depicting semaphore, I guess. Miranda has a longing to mix with the eternal and the symbolic but it requires too much steadfastness. So, she jumps from one thing to the next. She wasn't always this keen on Catholicism, you know. Six months ago it was the Taoists and six months hence, who knows, she might be down at the Kingdom Hall, doing whatever they do there."

Charlie is scathingly critical of Miranda, and I have grown

accustomed to his opinions. I come to her defense lamely, with comments such as, "Well, she seems to be true to herself," or, "She's very independent," while Charlie sniffs and snorts and takes swigs of fish emulsion.

I wonder if Richard would like her. I know that she is irresponsible and self-absorbed, but she has a directness about her, a kind of honesty of the heart, which I like. Joel would detest her.

Speaking of whom, a letter arrived on Friday and this is all he had to say. "Love from one being to the other can only be that two solitudes come nearer, recognize and protect and comfort each other. Han Suyin. It's the recognizing part that you fall down in, Gayle. Good-bye, Joel."

Maybe he is correct. I am so preoccupied with my attraction to Miranda, I forget why I am here. My interest in her is a kind of fugue, a flight from another flight, because daily I think of returning to Joel and Richard. And at least once every day I experience that feeling of being so far from home and so misguided by my motives and so wrong in my actions, that the wind is knocked from my lungs and I cannot breathe properly. My chest is constricted by a vague embarrassment.

But when night falls, I seem to relax, as if the darkness has allowed me to exhale more completely and I lean back and observe the windows of this village, and the hills and ocean, and Miranda, without apprehension. It is then that this future here on Lantau Island becomes the only one of any importance to me and I want to stay. It is easy to forget about the existence of airlines and the possibility of international travel and going back. It is easy to imagine that it is very necessary for me to stay here, very necessary for me to seduce Miranda, and only a little necessary for me to get my answers from Elizabeth. And so I stay, and admire my new camera strap, and go on hikes.

This morning it was very early when we left and our voices cast out around us, awakening dogs and chickens. We followed the longer route to Charlie's, past the island's most opulent home, owned by a businessman who is rarely there. "He has an artist girlfriend," Miranda told me as we stood in the yard. "I think he has a wife, too, in a house in the city. Once, when I was walking by last summer on my way to Charlie's house, I came across her, the girlfriend that is, and a model. She was sitting in the orchard, on a chair, naked, and the girlfriend-artist was drawing her."

"It was one of those perfect moments, you know," Miranda said to me. "They happen once in a while when all of the usual messiness of life gets held at bay somehow for a moment and the result is . . . beauty, I guess, flawlessness." Then she looked at me and said, "My life is messy isn't it? Wouldn't you agree that it's a perfect mess?"

There was no sign of life at the house, so Elizabeth had gone up close to one of the windows, then called to us to come and peek inside. The floors were black and white tile and the furniture mahogany. The rooms had the restful quality wealth bestows, the coolness and light of thoughtful design. "It's like the lobby of the Sunning House Hotel," Miranda said. I did not comment, not wishing to hear of her experiences at this, or any other, hotel in Hong Kong.

Jocelyn and Willy were anxious to keep moving, so we hurried downhill to Charlie and Pui Sin's house. From a distance, already we could see Pui Sin going into and out of the house, and when we arrived, there was Charlie frying ginger and tofu in oil. (Joel would be appalled at the amount of frying that goes on here, the intentional corking up of arteries, as he would see it.)

Charlie had moved his poster of Sun Yat-sen to the kitchen and insisted that everyone admire it. He goes to great trouble with his posters, gluing them on to cardboard backing and attaching hangers to them. In the background was Peking in winter, and Elizabeth commented that it had been a long time since she had seen, or even thought of, snow.

Charlie asked, "What are we all doing here, living on the Tropic of Cancer? It will be 1997 soon enough, the lease is running out. Plans, we need plans. Something I have always wanted to do is take the train across Russia. We could, you know. This winter. I have money enough for all of us. See Lake Baykal, Novosibirsk, Omsk and so on and so forth. There's a spur line to Tashkent; if the authorities didn't mind, we could go. They're all liberal-minded now, what with perestroika and glasnost. Think about waking to snow falling on the Russian plains."

"I'm game," Elizabeth said. "I'll be going back to Canada sometime and that would be the ideal route. I even know a bit of Russian. How to ask for coffee with milk, for instance, or how to say 'I don't know,'" and looking at Charlie, Elizabeth said, "*Ya nee znayoo.*"

"*Ya nee znayoo,*" Charlie repeated.

And I said, "You would fit right in on the train, Elizabeth. There would be all sorts of rural people, communards, or maybe they don't call themselves that anymore. They might have bags of flour and tea or oats or flax, you know, staples. The products that are always shown in school atlases. You could ask them exactly what they are thinking now of Marx and Engels."

Elizabeth thought that I was making fun of her, which I was not, and responded rather sarcastically by saying, "And you could question them on the fascinating topic of winter fallow." Sometimes we irritate one another, it seems.

Miranda said, "I love plains. But I think it would be better to visit Russia in summer. Then, it would be like crossing Australia, desert and grassland, I imagine. It's always seemed to me that it's the prairies and not the mountains that are the high ground or the holy ground. You know, the place where the spirits live. I think that spirits congregate on the plains and are hovering just above the earth. Not all types of spirits, of course, just certain ones. The wind-loving ones, I guess."

I wish Miranda would not talk like this in Charlie's presence, because there is always an uncomfortable silence afterward and Charlie's back manages most often to be turned to me and I imagine that he rolls his eyes or sucks in his cheeks disdainfully. To distract everyone, I felt compelled to jump in with my story of the turkeys, the prairie turkeys. I wanted them to know that because of my experience, I could never become overly romantic about prairies.

"I remember one summer day," I began, "when I was driving from Calgary to Constance, to the research station there. It's so flat in places along that highway and the horizon is so unchanged, I remember thinking that day that, in certain directions, it could be any century at all. I had a feeling of there being historical life all around me, buffalo and dinosaurs and even old lakes and the plants that had become oil. I went into a sort of trance, and then a very unsettling thing happened.

"There had been a truck way ahead of me, carrying turkeys, and I guess it must have hit a bump and one of the cage doors come ajar, because about a dozen turkeys had jumped out and landed on the highway. I stopped my car and got out, wanting to do something for them. They were so homely and pathetic, and even though they were injured, they were running around madly, heading out into the fields. I remember thinking, 'They're deranged.' Then, all of a sudden I became scared, really panicky, afraid of the openness, as if it were too liberal or something, too unpredictable. Too much scope for trouble. I felt completely unprotected, so I got inside my car and took off away from those turkeys."

I was a little carried away with myself, a little flushed and dizzy with the telling of this tale. My listeners had that slightly distorted, unnaturally looming look, the kind experienced just prior to fainting. I did not let on though, shook my head and said, "But the train might be different. I mean travelling by train across the prairies might be better, everything being held on to the tracks and so on."

Only Richard has ever understood the way I felt about the turkeys; I do not think anyone with me at the time of this telling did. I think they were actually glad when I stopped talking and Pui Sin took over.

She told us that she has been giving thought to leaving also, that she might move to Vancouver, not for political reasons, but to live with her daughter. She said that she was not afraid of the changes to come, that she had once been a member of the Red Guard, but had also lost a good friend during the Cultural Revolution because of some plays she had written. "I have always been of two minds about it all," she said, "and thought that when I became old it would become clear. Now, all that is clear to me is that a country is a very clever work of the imagination."

We were all quiet for a while after Pui Sin's comments, even Jocelyn and Willy who had been studying *National Geographics* in a corner of the living room. After eating a bit and drinking more coffee, we started off again, into the valley for a way. Pui Sin and Charlie and Elizabeth walked together, discussing a nascent political party called Meeting Point, and Miranda and the children and I lagged behind. Miranda began to tell me about the Sunning House Hotel where, as I had tried not to imagine, she and Maurice have gone in the afternoons from time to time.

"That's actually why I lost the last job," she said. "Too much time spent at the Sunning House, with Maurice, when I should have been answering the telephone and so on. Yes, it was a combination of the Sunning House Hotel and Maurice. I hold them responsible," she said, laughing.

"There's something I haven't told you," she went on. "The last time I was there with Maurice, last Saturday afternoon, after work," adding emphasis to the word *after*, "he told me he was leaving. He said he had a cousin in Thailand he wanted to see and furthermore, it was time for us to part, he declared, unilaterally, which was thoughtful of him, I thought. The thing is, he said good-bye and left, right then and there. That was it. I was left standing on the very filthy carpet, with a lot of what felt like dirt and grit under my bare feet."

"It all took place in room number thirty-three. We've always asked for that room, so that is where this little drama unfolded, room number thirty-three, the room that features a swollen bathroom door that catches on the sink so you have to squeeze yourself sideways into the bathroom. That's where I went to feel sorry for myself. I've always felt a little bit trapped in that bathroom, which is good I think now, because it gave me the ideal opportunity to picture Maurice vanishing, which is a trick I have to deal with vanishing lovers."

Miranda picked a weed from between her toes and said, "In my mind, I watched him arriving in Bangkok, his cousin meeting him, some pallid academic type, you know, pants just hanging where his ass should be, getting the bags, then going out on to the street to look for a cab. I pictured the cab, the cab-driver and Maurice's expression as he got inside. And, even better, I pictured none of me inside of him. I pictured that I was not present in his mind. And then, he went. The car disappeared into the traffic and he was gone and I had what I wanted of him but he had nothing of mine. I know it sounds a bit cold-blooded, but it works. I gather up my mind from the thraldom of relationships in this way."

"Thraldom?" I said. "You really think of relationships as a thraldom?"

"Yes," she said, "I do, for me. Well, actually, it's Gordon who thinks that of me and he's right. It's not such a bad state of affairs. We all have our particular task-masters or jailers. We get along with them comfortably most of the time. You have one or two thraldoms of your own, no doubt."

"No doubt," I agreed happily, pleased with the loss of Maurice.

We walked through dense plant life along the valley floor and caught up with the others in a small clearing where Charlie said he comes to do his setting up exercises in the morning. There ensued a conversation about the meaning of setting up exercises, and Miranda and Willy reminisced about Babar the elephant and the lady in the city who took him in and gave him her wallet. Apparently that lady, too, did setting up exercises. We all agreed that we would like to meet such an old lady.

Then it was uphill to a cliff with a steep path similar to the cat-walk at home, which we crab-walked down to its base and a lovely, isolated beach. Standing at various spots, we changed into our bathing suits and swam and played and lay on towels in the sun. I was reminded of the relaxation exercises Joel used to encourage me to do when I could not sleep.

Elizabeth began to talk about Miss Peirce again, wanting to return to the counties and county towns and have Charlie recall everything he knew about such names as Middlesex, but he said "No, too tired." Undaunted, Elizabeth went on to do several impressions of our former teacher and her students. Stanley Ferris – I remember him, he had big hips and thighs – did not know the months of the year in grade eight. According to Elizabeth, he placed November after August, then fell apart completely under Miss Peirce's incredulous eyes. He cried and Miss Peirce became more hysterical than usual, predicting an era of complete incompetence, when fools who could not even reliably identify the season would be in charge of municipal duties such as the dispatch of snow clearing machinery.

I laughed as I lay on my back, but I did not watch Elizabeth. I watched the sky instead and left them all behind for a while, entering my own place of recall, a room, the classroom we once shared with our Miss Peirce. I remembered being with her in January of 1969, when it was very snowy and cold outside of those windows but inside, warm enough to wear those short-sleeved shirts of Dad's. I had my English grammar text on the desk. The exercises always went from "a" to "j"; always there were ten sentences to parse, unlikely groups of words such as, "Unfortunately, the lapidarist's gems had gone missing in Brazil." We underlined and drew arrows and thought "subjective completion" and so on.

For a while, I had the habit of adding a "k," "Your father regrets."

I would circle “father,” draw an arrow from it to “your,” underline “regrets” twice and draw another arrow to the white space between the blue lines of my notebook, thinking that this indicated that he was still somewhere between the earth and the sky. Then, I would quickly erase it all.

One day, however, I did not erase it quickly enough, and Miss Peirce, seeing that I had made an addition to the exercise, picked up my scribbler and opened her mouth to speak. Upon reading the words though, she stopped herself, returned the book to my desk and looked at me in a way that seemed to question the integrity of my pain, in a way that seemed to suggest that Duncan McDonagh had been crazy anyway. I hated her at that moment and the intensity of that hatred returned to me as I lay there, lopping me off from the others in a greedy and exquisite way. My very own bone to chew on while everyone else starved.

We stayed for most of the afternoon and for the trip home I walked behind the children and Miranda, watching her feet flip-flopping in the earth and her legs above them. In some ways, it is just like Alberta here. There are times when, judging by the scenery, it could be any century at all.

Richard

Richard, Richard, Richard, he said to himself in the bathroom mirror. Your demeanor belies the facts. It is like Mr. Neville's house was back in Unity, with its attractive gingerbreading and gabled roof and no hint of the fact that its owner was prowling the town by night, stealing garden hoses, spades, rakes, snow shovels and even Christmas wreaths. No one knew until Mr. Neville died, which was a tribute to his ghostly stealth. When his basement was cleaned out, there were enough yard and home accessories to cover his, and his neighbour's, lawn. The whole town came by to claim lost possessions. It was a big story in the *Informer*, one of the biggest ever.

And now, Richard thought, years later, my face is very much like that house. Only Margaret Bain suspects that there is something going on, although I have changed my habits and photocopy mostly during my lunch hour now, he said to himself. Still, she is wise to me. She watches my comings and goings and she is a stern observer. Her posture is so erect, her body so perfectly odourless, her clothing so elegantly draped around her, and of such good quality, that Richard suspected Margaret had never known an inappropriate thought in her life, let alone swindled the library out of its resources. There was nothing in that mind that could not come out under oath, let us say, at some sort of campus inquiry into wrongdoings. Richard imagined Margaret speaking clearly and forthrightly into a microphone to say that, yes, on occasion she had considered taking reference material home for personal use but, on second thought, had never actually done so. Assorted deans and academic vice-presidents would watch with satisfaction and a certain fulfilment.

Richard stopped himself from thinking further in this direction and returned to his kitchen where he had been cleaning cupboards. There his face was reflected in the concave silver knobs, and the distortion seemed more representative than the smooth, mirror image in the bathroom had been. Richard put his arms around Reba's neck and the two of them looked into a knob together.

The cupboards were filled with food bought in bulk from an alternative store where the flour and rice and split peas and barley were kept in large barrels with wooden lids. Richard purchased bags full and kept them thus packaged until the inevitable infestation of the merchant grain beetles occurred. Then, he cleared it all away, throwing the bags of bulgur and bran and rolled oats into the garbage and setting the jars of figs and lentils and dried soup mix onto a chair, so as to contemplate their use.

It is a subterfuge, Richard thought as he cleaned, owning these grains and so on, it is an artifice. How often do I make tabbouli or the twenty minute kind of porridge or even bran muffins? Never, in fact. This is simply a storing up of the unrefined and heavy foods which I, for some reason, believe will be completing to me, fill up all of the nutritional emptinesses. Or, maybe dislodge all of the fatty, clinging residue and exhaust it into the toilet. That is what the barley green was intended to do.

Richard stood and, to his grocery list, added Cheerios and instant biscuit mix. He saw this as abandoning the idea of an inner cleanliness. He saw this as an intention to litter and clog his gastro-intestinal tract in much the same way he had his apartment.

After everything had been removed from the cupboards, Richard swept out the mouse turds and the dead ants and the grains of rice. There was, in the very back, yet another bag of flour containing the beetles' serpentine trails of life. It pleased Richard to think of them burrowing through whiteness. He was reminded of his job, the stacks of paper, and himself wandering amidst them with, no doubt, some aim housed in his glands or, as Joel would say, his hindbrain, the tiny parts of him which when cross-sectioned and laid out on a microscope slide would look disturbingly similar to the merchant grain beetle's parts.

Richard put away the insecticide recommended for swabbing away all traces of insect life and decided to wash out the interior of his cupboards with clear water. Reba watched and licked once at the bucket. Then Richard said, "I'll pack the soybeans and the yogurt container of rosemary and the alfalfa seeds and the lentils and the dried soup mix and the pinto beans into my green bag and we'll cart them over to the food bank. There must be someone who wants this stuff."

Before going out, Richard surveyed the peaceful and less explicit squalor evening light bestowed upon his apartment. There were his papers spread over the living room floor, beneath the rocking chair and coffee table and on top of the couch with its cigarette burn. Even Reba tried to walk around them now as they sat in piles, waiting to be skimmed and highlighted with the yellow marker. The backlog did not prevent Richard from wanting more Brieflies, more articles, more evidence, and this insatiable desire kept him going, made him alternately gleeful and aghast at his glee. Today, he was more inclined to be aghast as he closed the door behind him.

They walked across the Louise Bridge. With the sun just setting, the mountains were dark with brilliant borders, the way one expects visions to be, in ecstatic moments, if our minds and lives could only be synchronized in a more poetic fashion, Richard thought. He turned his head to look at the downtown structures and wished for one that would neither reflect nor be opaque, but rather be transparent glass so that one might see, working late, some tireless businessperson of the old-fashioned school such as might be seen in the Chrysler Building; a person who could, perhaps, be a superhero. Nowadays we can never see what is going on inside those buildings, Richard thought; they cause the viewer to feel rejected.

Richard had not seen anyone socially for fifteen days, and the sight of those cold and imposing office towers aroused in him a knowledge of wanting something, a camaraderie, if only of onlookers and sitters like himself. He decided to walk through the bus depot on his way to the food bank. It was only a little way off his route and there would be talk and announcements and an atmosphere of modest anticipation.

At the depot there were all manner of people, old men in suits of a European cut, young women in sweaters with V-necks and chains, middle-aged women crocheting squares, and the very old, both men and women, wearing all-weather coats against the warm evening. Richard was very pleased with all of them. He stood and concentrated on a woman walking a line from the ladies' washroom door to the phones and back again. There was a quality to her gait and her startled, withheld movements that suggested to Richard that this woman was not average. He remembered then that he had seen her before, downtown on the mall, tap dancing for donations.

As Richard watched her with her three bags, prepared for travel, he began to think that someone should be congratulated upon this feat of organization, someone should be given an award for this improbable bringing together of bus schedules and the tap dancer's wayward life so that they could mate to some end. It was almost miraculous, Richard thought, laughing to himself. He was happy, thinking of the bus drivers and the buses and all of their many contingencies of double shifts and weekends and overtime and maintenance, oil and fluid and brakes, and the whirling dervish of this woman's life, skittering here and there, with no course charted. How could they have managed to unite in this way? And not only was she there, and a bus to transport her, but somewhere, elsewhere, another set of circumstances, people and machinery and history, awaited her, a gnarl of connections along a secondary road probably, somewhere in rural Alberta. It was all far better than astrology, Richard said to himself.

Richard wanted to talk to this woman, but her behaviour, buzzing to a door here and a locker there, as if in search of some long-lost quality, such as stability or permanence, recommended a slow approach. He drew near to her resting place by the telephones and stood for a while, pretending to take a locker. "Going north?" Richard asked, after what he thought was a suitable wait.

She spoke up immediately and with no hesitation, continuing to scan the room with her eyes. "Yes, to Innisfail. Then I change to the Bailey Bus Lines. They go through Abner, Halo, all those whistle stops along the 23. I get off at Mignon. You know Mignon?"

"No, I don't I'm afraid," Richard answered.

"I have a sister there," the woman said, and then, as if this short exchange had had a push and a scare to it, she paced quickly to the washroom door, looked in and returned. Coming closer to Richard and glancing downward, she said, "Those are big feet you've got yourself there." Then, "Heh, heh," she laughed to herself while peering into an empty locker.

"Good for walking. I don't drive a car. My name's Richard, by the way."

"Oh, my sister's name is Yvonne," said the woman with surprise in her voice, as if Richard and Yvonne were historically or coincidentally related, like Romeo and Juliet or Adam and Eve. She never did divulge her own name, but Richard decided that parents who had named one daughter Yvonne had probably named another Evelyn. So, that is how he thought of her.

Evelyn flinched a couple of times, as if watching a fight or hearing blows, then smiled up at Richard, saying, "I hear a great big container of some chemical sank off the coast of France. They say it'll be big trouble if it breaks and gets into the water. Bad fish, less oxygen. Breathing gets harder every day, don't you find? I notice if I just stick my nose into one of these lockers I get a better breath. It's not so used up. I read a while ago that there's a very strong likelihood that you or I, in the next couple of days, will breathe in a molecule of oxygen, I mean an identical same molecule, as was breathed in, and out of course, by Julius Caesar. It's hard to believe." She paused then said, "You can't see air, but it's changing all the time in ways that make it harder to breathe. It's hard to know which is better, inside or outside. The people in India – that place, Bhopal – who stayed inside were better off, but I like to be outside as much as I can. You can smell the diesel fumes in here. Yvonne's house has bacon smells in it from five years ago when Bud was still alive. My room's in a basement but there are two windows right at ground level which is best as far as I'm concerned because the grass and weeds grow right up to the window ledge and they shoot the oxygen right into my room."

"You must read the newspaper a lot," Richard commented.

"I do," Evelyn said. "Every day. First thing," then she hurried over to one of the exits and squinted skyward. When Evelyn returned she said, "No sign of anything."

"Good," said Richard.

Her bus was called, gate seven to Red Deer. Richard carried two of Evelyn's bags the length of the depot and they said goodbye. Reba was overjoyed to be outside again.

The food bank was close by, but by the time they arrived it was almost nine o'clock and the volunteer on duty was anxious to close. Taking one look at the contents of Richard's bag, he said, "We can't accept that stuff. It has to be packaged, you know, all sealed up like this," and he held up a can of peaches and a bag of macaroni noodles. "You know, someone might have tampered with it, cyanide, razor blades, that kind of thing."

Richard began to wonder if he looked crazy and grizzled after all, maybe not as neutral as Mr. Neville, but suspicious, devious, questionable or secretly vicious. Turned away from donating at the food bank, he thought, I have achieved a philanthropic nadir. Rethinking it all, however, he realized that traces of beetle life might very well exist in some of his jars, and he wondered what sort of marginal group this placed him within. He recalled a line from a pamphlet on scabies he had read some months ago while in his doctor's waiting room. "Minimal standards of hygiene are all that is necessary to prevent outbreak." Outside, opening the jars, expecting armies of insects and whitish clumps of larvae to fall out, he contemplated minimal standards and asked himself if they had perhaps slipped beyond his grasp.

No bugs to be seen, and that was a relief. Still, it was satisfying to throw the jars, one by one, into the garbage dumpster, fling them hard, so that the glass would be certain to break.

Gayle

I am sitting on the beach thinking about Richard and Dad and Mother and the way things used to be. It is overcast and hot and claustrophobically humid, as if some power were forcing heavy, wet air into the too-small space beneath the foggy sky. It is a day like the day Mom pointed the collander at me, the kind of day that Richard would have spent playing Hi-Q when we were kids, trying over and over again for the genius category, one red plastic peg in the centre of the board. It is the kind of day that provokes exasperation.

I think that exasperation occurs when a person realizes, fully, that another person is another person; that even though you may have lived with this person for years, or even spawned this other person, the realization hits, finally, that the skin is a closed and absolutely sealed covering. It circles around the body with the deceptive twists of the Mobius strip, so that we are led to believe an entrance must exist, a place which can be folded back to break the continuity. But no. There are no gaps to allow passage from one to another. Although parents and lovers must live in the hope of such a possibility.

At the time of the collander incident, Mom was involved with that study group, I believe, investigating the problems and advantages of everyday life in a socialist state. Maybe her exasperation was related to that. Many times a day she would point out to us how conditions would differ if we lived in Cuba or the USSR, that Chiclets would be unavailable to us, or that there would be no hockey coins in Jell-O packages and no collector trays to send for. That sort of excess annoyed her. I can still hear her saying, "I don't think any of you would last a day in a socialist society."

Richard must have been upstairs with the Hi-Q game that day, because only Dad and I were downstairs with Mom. We were drinking grape pop and reading novels in the big vinyl chair. Actually, he was sitting in it with his legs stretched out in a V and I was sitting between his legs with my arms resting on his knees, the way we sometimes did. He was jolly and lazy that day and I remember noticing that his hair was longer and curlier than I had ever seen it. I thought that he was beginning to look like one of the twelve disciples or one of the Rolling Stones.

It must have been August, I don't know what year, but Mom was harvesting from the garden and, no doubt, there were crops Dad was letting stand past their prime. It had been spitting rain; nevertheless, Mom had picked some peas and come back inside with her arms spattered in mud, leaving her heavy boots outside the screen door. The screen was covered with mosquitoes whining and sawing with their snouts. Mom shelled peas at a frantic rate and when the radio announcer said, "At the sound of the tone it will be exactly one o'clock, eastern daylight saving time," it became apparent that she was angry, so much tearing and hurling of pods during the brief silence before the time signal. I looked up. She finished the peas and plunged back into the garden for more produce.

When Mom returned, she had a basket of beans which she scraped across the countertop before beginning a clattering search through the pots and pans. That is when, without warning, she whirled around and, pointing at Dad and me with the collander, announced that she had had enough. At first it was the laziness of us all, the lack of productivity; her complaints were purely economical. Then she stopped, looking as if she would let it all drop, as she had on so many occasions, but she must have changed her mind. Her face darkened and the collander jabbed above me, looking like a sputnik, and Mom said, "And you, for a girl of your age to be snuggled up to a book, and your father, while your mother does all the work, well, it's a shame. That's all I can say. Shame on you. Shame on you both." And with that she began furiously collecting the empty pop bottles and dropping them into a cardboard container.

Dad hoisted one leg up over my head and said, "Well, maybe I should wander out to the barn. Must be something that needs doing."

I went outside and walked to the swamp, in my shorts, wearing thongs on my feet. The frogs stopped singing as they heard my approach, but I sat among the weeds and bulrushes until they began again. From that time onward, I decided, I would sit in the rocking chair to read, which I did.

It is so grey here today, grey sky meets grey water. And all of these people walking up and down the beach in their stretched and separate skins (restless because today is a holiday and there is no sunlight) only serve to make me feel impatient and want something, Miranda I guess it is, more.

I have bought us two canvas beach chairs which are very similar to the two Richard and I used to leave on the beach, beneath the overturned rowboat. After dinner we carry them to the water's edge to sit and watch Jocelyn and Willy; there is usually enough light from the village and the moon to make swimming safe. Such a pleasant way to end the day. The sound of the water is like a repetitive and soothing brushing, as if with each wave the colour of the sky were supplanted by another darker shade, slowly acquiescing to the night. Even our talk is fluid now, it seems. We set up our chairs and it ebbs between us.

I have been telling Miranda about some of the people Joel has worked with, the man with sinesthesia, for example. I told her about the confusion of dimensions, taking roast pork to be rectangular or fish smells to be a trapezoid. I remembered that he used to compliment Joel when he wore a certain green shirt, telling him it was a perfect F-sharp from an oboe. Miranda wanted to know more about him, wanted to know if, as he took in more and more sounds and sights, they became woven and bundled together until he achieved a type of contemplative experience. Then, without waiting for my response, she said that once when she was having Willy's ears tested, the audiologist had invited her to look through the instrument to Willy's eardrums. She said, "Have you ever seen an eardrum? It's gorgeous, really, white, almost transparent. Like a shell. And then there are all those tools behind it, hammers and anvils and so on working and vibrating and causing understanding to occur. I just wonder if that would happen for him in a different way. Do you know what I mean?"

"I mean," she went on, "would he run up against a point like that, a big ear drum sort of experience, a point at which it was all collected and made sense of but without the usual system of words and air waves? Sort of like transcendental meditation. Maybe you could ask him when you go back."

And that is what I wanted to dwell upon about this conversation, the phrase "when you go back." It was that asymmetric moment again, a mismatch of sensation to hear her say in such a neutral voice, "When you go back," as if she were saying, "When you pick up the mail," or "When you go to the drugstore."

However, as I sit here now, I imagine myself back in Canada and the trip to Roy's Camera Shop where I know the sinesthesic is employed, and the questions I could ask to satisfy Miranda. And then the letter I would write, the composing of which would bring such percussion to my evening that I would not be able to sleep, and next day, would have to lie down in the garden (presuming they would re-hire me, which they probably would not) at noon, and sleep with my face in the earth.

These "when you get back" tremors are my own fault, I suppose. I sit next to Miranda and I am compelled to talk to her, telling her the most uninteresting details from my past. I often feel while I talk to her that I am walking closer and closer to some dilated and beckoning place, some place too high, where blood might gush from my nose and fall warmly into the cupped hands which I could hold up to her, saying "Look at this."

Am I a fool? Possibly.

I told her about the garden in Vancouver, about breathing in the arbutus bark and snails and fungus and how these had seemed to me to be all the ingredients needed to produce anything lively. I told her how much I enjoyed pushing my face right into the forest floor there, right into the yeasty bubblings of the earth. And Miranda, watching Willy and Jocelyn race one another under water, said to me rather coyly, "It sounds like sniffing underwear to me. Does this mean that you like to smell your underwear too, then, on top of all of your other perversions? After you've worn it, I mean?"

I said, "No," then, "Well, actually, yes, once in a while."

Miranda laughed and said, "You didn't want to admit to that, did you?"

I looked at the water and she looked at me and there followed a moment of embarrassed intimacy. Still, it was intimacy, the way intimacy can be, for two sets of eyes only, as if we had both looked along the beach and seen the same improbable vision, a herd of cretaceous horses no bigger than foxes or a school of human babies swimming to shore.

The moment did not last for long. Willy held Jocelyn under water and Miranda shouted, "Willy, stop it or you can come out right now." She walked to the water's edge and Jocelyn emerged, sputtering and crying and accusing, and went to Miranda who wrapped her in a towel and came to collect her chair. The two of them walked to the apartment. Willy stayed with me and swam while I felt the warmth of the sand radiate upward. I had the feeling that unpredictable organic activity was occurring just beneath the surface, that if I dug only an inch or two I would uncover lilies or hyacinths. I imagine too much, I know that is what Joel would say, but I am not completely deluded, because since that day Miranda has begun to pay a different kind of attention to me.

Yesterday, in the afternoon, I was sitting on the balcony, trying to re-discover my neglected ability to do botanical drawings. All of life was clattering and spraying outside beneath the balcony, dragging bricks here and there and cooking. The communists on our south side had moved their record player to the roof and were playing their records again, while the storekeeper across the way stood in the street with arms crossed, watching the communists' roof for signs of collectivism, as if it might spill down the walls and wash away his Ribena display.

Into the midst of my drawing and observation came Miranda.

She said, "I didn't know you could draw," and I do believe that it was at that moment that a vague premeditation began for her. She may not have thought the words, but there was a certain conducting of information via the blood's seductive momentum.

"Let's walk to the businessman's garden," she said. "We can take our chairs and paper and pencils and draw."

A warning word dropped inside me, thousands and thousands of miles and finally out of sight. I have no idea what it was.

"Sure," I said. "It would be beautiful there today."

As we walked I recognized a reciprocity in Miranda, for the first time, evidence of "maybe" in her speech. Halfway there, she said, "I have to pee," and disappeared into the plant life while I waited and concentrated on the village below us with its distant dog and hammer noises. There was a melancholy and confined ring to them, as if prohibited from too much movement by the smoky haze thrown up by village life.

We climbed upward. When we arrived Miranda said, "You put your chair there and I'll sit over here." Then, from about twenty paces, without even turning to look at me, she asked, "Do you mind taking your clothes off?"

I had a sudden burst of anxiety, noise in my mind like several busy and crowded situations, banquets and intersections all rolled into one harsh bray, and then nothing, silence. "Of course not," I said, "that is, I don't mind at all." This was almost a complete lie.

After I had folded my clothes and placed them neatly beneath the chair, I sat myself down and studied the trees of the orchard so as to avoid Miranda's gaze. While she drew I had an expectation that hidden among the boughs of the fruit trees was a choir and that, at any moment, two or three hundred voices would call out in one wild, soprano, opening note. I anticipated some sort of oratorio from the shrubs and flower beds, a celebratory motif which spoke earnestly of my desire. That was my state.

Miranda drew for perhaps half an hour and at last said, "Here it is. Take a look."

The banquet and intersection noises rose again, and I wondered, with my clothes? without my clothes? and, as the sounds abated, I dressed and heard Miranda laugh to herself. I told her I would not look just then, but would draw her instead.

She undressed with complete casualness and looked at me

from her chair with no shyness whatsoever. I could not have in the least begun to represent her on paper, so chose to draw the orange tree beneath which she sat, and became very absorbed in the beauty of it with Miranda's white and smiling and wild-haired self beneath. It would have made a very pleasing black and white photograph. I would like to possess such an image right now, to admire from where I sit on this wet beach. Her legs were crossed and her foot twitched and moved impatiently at times. As I drew, I was aware again of the noises of the village, still pleasantly contained and muffled by its own vapours.

I completed my tree rather hastily and displayed it to Miranda, walked up close to her in her canvas chair, quite brazenly I thought, and she smiled at me. Her breasts were rounder and fuller than I had imagined and I wondered if she were still nursing Jocelyn and Willy. Nothing is out of the question, where Miranda is concerned.

I asked what she had been thinking while I drew and she said she was remembering a time in high school when they were learning map reading. Everyone had departed from different points, with a map created by the geography teacher, but was expected to meet later in the afternoon at the same destination, a campground. Miranda had misinterpreted her map and waited at an abandoned farmhouse for hours while her classmates ate hot dogs and played soccer. She said, ever since then, she has worried about having misunderstood, or misread, or overlooked, the most significant information. Then she began to cry, not sobs, only a few tears. I touched her head and said, "We should go home. The kids will be there soon."

On the way home Miranda asked if I would hold her hand. "Jocelyn won't, you know. She thinks I'm ill."

We held hands as we walked. It was mossy under foot until we reached the village with its raging television sets and hanging fabric and crates upon crates upon crates. I bought us each a beer from the communists, which we drank, and then I slipped off to Charlie and Pui Sin's for the evening. I wanted to get away for a while.

That was last night. And now here I sit on the beach, reminded by the imperceptible and grey union of sea and sky, of Miranda, and her flawless, continuous skin.

Richard

Richard was looking at his calendar. He liked to lift the page and peek ahead to September, even though there were absolutely no engagements pencilled in on it, or October. The pages' glossy emptiness formed a neat package, Richard thought, with his unplugged telephone atop the fridge, a set of disconnections. He was actually thinking of returning his telephone to the Alberta Government Telephone Company and using the phone booth outside the Blue Jay Variety to make calls, having as his goal the reduction of unexpected sound in his apartment to almost zero. Richard was able to accept that Reba's occasional barking could not be prevented.

Overall, at his home, circumstances seemed to be improving and, ironically, this pleased Richard in the way a very thorough house-cleaning will, despite the steady growth of untidiness and disorganization. It was at work where the trouble remained, where the comings and goings, the observations and questions of Margaret Bain, were bothersome. Only three days ago she had asked Richard if he wanted some time off. "No," he had answered testily, then proceeded to wonder if he were psychologically transparent, if he were developing the stretched facial expression Lisa Lemire had acquired before running amok on the fifth floor and shouting "cocksuckers!" at the top of her voice. No, he reassured himself, he was not at all like Lisa, who had been smiling wanly for weeks before her rampage. Why, he had consciously assumed a look of amusement and candour, the expression of a sort of bookish bon vivant, especially in his dealings with Margaret. That was how he kept her at bay.

Richard knew about the "Helping in Crisis" skills Margaret had acquired after the Lemire debacle. Just the day before, while he searched through back issues of the *Winnipeg Free Press* on microfiche, she had approached him, he knew, with the intent to intervene, to communicate, to mention the services of the Employee Assistance Programme. But he had cut her off at the pass.

"I do need to familiarize myself with all of the resources available on this floor," Richard had said with gusto. "So many history students come through here at a complete loss."

"How are those student handouts coming along?" she had asked, with an emphasis on the word *are* which Richard took to denote patronizing disbelief. This spurred him on.

"When I've finished with this newspaper survey, I should have something concrete for you," had been Richard's reply, his eyes shining with the joy of successful deception.

Margaret had made no comment regarding the newspaper survey, and because of this Richard wondered, later, if she were perhaps becoming frightened of him. He began to feel a worried hopefulness that someday soon, on the fifth floor, he would be left entirely to his own devices, that colleagues and supervisors alike would shun him out of a nervous deference to his mute searchings.

Richard realized that the level of inappropriateness of his behaviour had escalated. Reference material had become less interesting than newspapers, and, instead of photocopying, he now printed on the microfiche copier pieces of interest from the newspapers of the fifties, sixties and seventies. No one except Margaret had, as yet, interrupted him at this work. Who would, after all? No one had stood in the way of Lisa Lemire.

Should I worry? Richard wondered, as he thought before the calendar. Should I worry about work and Margaret Bain and the calendar's pages? he asked himself earnestly. He was feeling a bit unguided, he had to admit. The days were becoming more and more unstructured, in the way the turning of the earth had possibly intended them to be, unaffected by human plans. But surely it was not right to have the minutes rolling by entirely without navigation, like the clouds in the sky. He no longer was aware even of the grimness of any portion of the day, and wondered if this phenomenon had vanished or become obscured by its ubiquitousness. For a time, he had been able to judge from the faces of the people on the bus. In the mornings they had often appeared to be melting in the sunlight, loosening and sagging from their skulls. By late afternoon, however, they had become soft and secretive, heading home to the secure moorings Richard had imagined for them. Of late, he had ceased to notice the whole lot of them in the morning, so preoccupied was he with thoughts of Margaret and his newspapers. And after work, Richard had taken to walking home.

Yes, the calendar's pages could maybe set things straight for him. It was like staring at the night sky, Richard thought, wrapping the firmament into numbered squares so that a direction could be charted. Looking at Reba, Richard said with resolve, "This is the schedule," and taking the calendar from the wall, sat down with his tea and tried to impose plans on the remainder of August. He began by printing "walk home" on each of the days of the approaching work week. That would take care of physical exercise. Then, he printed "martini" beneath "walk home" on Thursday and Friday, and "tea" on Monday, Tuesday and Wednesday. Richard felt that that was a good beginning and deserving of a rest break.

There were two items in Richard's pocket from the *Winnipeg Free Press*, October 1967, which he read for the second time. One concerned a wrecking ball which had come free and crushed the roof of a man's car. "I'm just glad I wasn't in it," Leo Pelletier was quoted as saying. The other had to do with an ammonia leak in a TV dinner factory. One woman had died and two others had succumbed to the fumes but were later revived. It was not known if either would suffer any long-term damage. Richard wondered if they had and wished there were some way he could find out.

Richard was unsure where to place these bits of paper. He had categorized his stores of information to a degree so that there was a section on nervous and mental diseases for Joel, beneath his coffee table, and an astronomy file which Richard called "irrefutable evidence," near his rocking chair. In front of the television were genetic anomalies and beneath the window, social anthropology. The Brieflies were scattered everywhere, in no scheme whatsoever, which was irksome, really. And now that he was feeling more comfortable in his own home, Richard decided that it was time to retrieve some floor space and begin a process of filing and stacking.

What Richard needed was a large box. He went directly to his closet shelf and located the Hiram and Walker box full of *Informers*, thinking, "I should at least go through these for the interesting parts before I throw them out." Sitting down with the box, Richard flipped its contents onto the couch and there, at what had been the bottom of the pile, was the headline "Local Farmer Disappears." Very large, black, capital letters had been used, the size of print which might be chosen to announce the reinstatement of the death penalty or the assassination of the prime minister.

For a moment, those three bold words made no sense at all, although Richard read them to himself, then spoke them aloud. It was as if he had temporarily lost the ability to use or understand the symbols of language. They seemed to him to be fracturing into their component curves and lines, disintegrating into another form; they looked like chromosomes on the loose searching for fraternity, wanting, with a drive like sexual desire, to create a new significance, a different type of meaning. "This must be what talking in tongues is like," Richard thought for the moment before the letters and sounds joined together again to make sense.

"Local Farmer Disappears," Richard then read, "by Iris Chesney."

"Unity police were notified early Friday morning that Duncan McDonagh, 55, of the twelfth concession, had been missing since the previous night. As of today, his whereabouts remain a mystery.

"Mr. McDonagh was last seen the evening of Wednesday, December fourth. Mrs. McDonagh has told police that her husband spent that evening with his family. Mr. and Mrs. McDonagh have two children, twins, Richard and Gayle, aged twelve.

"Louise McDonagh, known to many for her involvement in service groups and last year's centennial project, has been assisting police in the organization of search parties. She told the *Informer* this morning that her husband often goes walking along the lake shore and in the woods and, she fears, may have met with an accident of some sort.

"Anyone wishing to help in the search is asked to call the Unity detachment of the Ontario Provincial Police."

Lots of people had helped, Richard recalled, plenty of people. They had walked the cat-walk to the beach and up and down in groups of black coats, it had seemed. Then, one by one, they had disappeared into the trees, calling "Duncan, Duncan." The far off snapping of branches had sounded like wood fire and had had some optimism to it. Richard and Gayle were told to stay home, but they had often followed.

The searching continued daily until Christmas, at which time the police called off the neighbourhood hunts. Then had come Christmas day, a miscreant event, a day of parcels and eating and an inescapable awareness that time had come and gone. Aunt Peg had taken Richard and Gayle to church that morning where Reverend Oke had recited a lengthy prayer for the safe homecoming of Duncan McDonagh, and Elaine Wheeler had placed her hand, with its lacquered nails, upon Richard's forearm and, without speaking, given it a little squeeze. Richard could remember most vividly feeling a terrible dismay at both the hard and steadfast reality of those fingernails, and the voodoo of prayer.

Richard and Gayle carried on their private searching throughout January, a bleak and unloving month, in the way that winter months with very little snow can be. The wind seemed to blow emptiness down their throats. Still, they expected to find him not too far away, maybe standing amid the grey and frozen goldenrod and yarrow, better, ready, with a new mood which could last for years.

After school it was very often close to dark, but Richard and Gayle made it a routine to check the Formans' sugar shack, believing it to be a possible base camp for their father's wanderings. If only they could catch him in. In the windowless shed, together they patted the walls and the floor with a terrifying and joyful certainty that he would be there, that their hands would rub against his jacket and his voice would start up again. "I have some new information on Stonehenge for you, doppelgangers," he might say.

In February, Constable Jordan had driven in the laneway with apocryphal tales of a man seen darting into the woods somewhere on the Bruce Peninsula. A Saturday afternoon was spent driving that winter-barren and tree-lined highway, Richard and Gayle taking turns with the binoculars, but no man was seen.

By March, Richard had found himself knowing that they must give up, colluding with necessity toward that end. Their homework was piling up; Miss Peirce followed a system of steaming through the math curriculum, with the most diligent students setting the pace. Every night at least five pages of exercises in math were assigned, along with grammar and composition and social studies. The little snow that had fallen was melting and the tramp to the sugar shack was becoming impossible. Mud caked to their boots and occasionally, in her haste, one of Gayle's feet would come free of its heavy boot and she would have to hop backwards to it on one foot, heavy as a Clydesdale. And as the countryside thawed, Gayle became filled with ideas for new places to search, the beaver dam, Duck Lake and the supposed underground passage behind the nuclear generating plant. Richard had listened and followed along with most.

Packing the papers back into the box, Richard recalled how one night, late in March, he had gone downstairs to make himself some hot milk. He had been wide awake, full of energy, and decided to go outside in boots and coat to drink. The weather had turned cold again and Richard was able to walk easily upon the frozen furrows. It was like stepping from shoulder blade to shoulder blade, he thought, as he walked out into the dark front field, holding his cup, absorbing the warmth from it.

There was no moon that night, only the sky full of its universe, too full for Richard to wish to contemplate. He watched the earth instead and came, unexpectedly, to the ring of stones his father had used as a fireplace for the questionable bonfires. Richard had sat imagining his father searching for the stones and placing them in that nearly perfect ring. He thought of him lighting fire after fire, alone, while he and Gayle had most likely been milking the cows and Louise had been at the Unity Municipal Building for one worthy reason or another.

It was as he scrutinized the fireplace that night that Richard had decided to look no further for Duncan McDonagh, and in so doing, discovered that the beginning of giving up, the beginning of the end of hope, can have a distinct quality of euphoria to it. He remembered wanting to tell Gayle this, but never doing so. Richard moved to his wheeled chair and sat recalling how he had cleared his mind that night, how he had begun thinking about the people further east, in Montreal and Halifax and St. John's, the people who were already up and about the day's business, those who were already in the sun's light. He had longed to be with them, any of them, in the midst of buses, and classrooms where French might be spoken, someplace where dogs were yelping, anywhere rather than in his parents' field of abandoned fireplaces and frozen plant life.

For the following few weeks after that, Richard repeatedly betrayed his sister. "I can't look now," he had said, "too much homework," or, "He must be so far away by now we could never find him," or, "I need a break." All of these, and other excuses, he had made to Gayle's unbelieving face.

She had carried on, in the white shirts of Duncan, until summer, at which time Louise had given the shirts and pants and most of their father's personal effects to the church for mission use. And Gayle was told that the searching must stop. Louise had had an embarrassment about her as she gave this order, but, nevertheless, after that things began to turn around.

In July, the cows were sold and portions of the barn renovated. Long rows of small cages, big enough for two hens each, were installed. Richard and Gayle were responsible for collecting the eggs which fell into a wire grating and rolled to a stop outside the cage. They used to like to dam up the water at the end of the bird-sized troughs until it almost overflowed.

Of course, in time it had become boring and arguments arose over who would do what and when. Richard had had the idea to post a schedule – Richard, Gayle, Richard, Gayle – and the appropriate day of the month next to each name. It was not that they could not remember who had done the job the day before, but that there were so many substitutions and omissions, due to other commitments or laziness, which needed to be recorded so that a tally could be made at the end of the month: Richard owes Gayle four, for example. Then the next month would have begun, Richard,

Richard, Richard, Richard.

It was a good schedule, Richard thought, a damn good schedule, because it had worked for years to resolve the conflicts surrounding hen care. What he was attempting to create now, he realized, admiring his calendar, was not at all the same. There was no sister, after all, to negotiate with, not even a girlfriend to harangue about dish-washing. But it satisfied Richard nonetheless, to tack it into the wall again and see, from across the room, on his rolling chair, instructions written on most of the days.

Gayle

I wish Richard were here. I think of calling him, telephoning to yesterday, but then he would seem even further away, hidden around behind the earth's back. And I do not like the idea of conversing with the past; I am too impatient today.

I can picture him so easily. He will be sitting in the late August heat, I suppose. It is dry there, I have heard. The irrigation systems will still be working in the south and in the east, graceful plumes visible from the roadside. They always remind me of those water-skiing ladies we once saw, with the white and turquoise feathers on their heads. And in the city, at the university and the garden, there will be hoses and darkened patches on walkways the people will step around, and the sound of firing sprinklers. There is certainly none of that on this island.

It is evening here. Maybe because it is evening, I have been day-dreaming about meeting Richard after work the way I used to, on the nights he stayed late, with plans to tell him everything. We could walk along beneath the tender bedtime whispering of the trees, among so much slanted motion and colour, to the pergola with the poplars overhead. We could talk. I could ask him questions.

What questions would I ask? I'll tell you. I would ask, "Richard, what is this life of the flesh? Or the passions? Or both sets of things? What is it all about?" But I wouldn't bother to wait for a reply.

Based upon my current experience, I would say, it is nearly all preparation. That very first intimacy is like preparing for a trip, packing and packing, imagining extra items which you must have and, at the last moment, when you are about ready to leave, beginning to believe that you are not quite ready after all. But it is too late. You are towed along, by your preparations, to a point where there is a little jolting forward and a little jolting backward, just like on the train. And although you never know really why that occurs, you do know what it means. No more waiting. It is the motion of no more waiting.

That is how it was when Miranda, without warning, entered my bedroom last night. She took off her clothes, exactly as she did in the businessman's garden, and lay down next to me. It was rather sudden and I was not prepared. I had not finished packing.

I had thought, I had imagined, that when and if we were to finally come together, there would at least have been background noise, the mah-jong tiles, voices and steam from the café downstairs, Elizabeth or the children talking in the next room. But outside there was only quiet. For some reason the entire village had shut down. I had the feeling they had all sucked in their breath and closed their eyes. There was not even light from the window, no moon, nothing, which, it was revealed to me, is the way Miranda likes it.

"I prefer total darkness," she said to me. "In the light, the other person seems tremendously far away from me." Miranda is one who finds it easy to use an abundance of adverbs.

I told her, as she lay there beside me, that one of the problems with no light, with being sightless, was that words seemed to want to crowd in to create sights for us. At least at that moment they did, because I was wanting to talk, I was wanting to show her some photographs, I was wanting to watch a movie with her, go on a date, have some sort of prelude.

I told her about the ancient Caldicott twins and their use of adverbs, about the time when, out of the blue and perhaps out of pity, they took Richard and me to the O'Keefe Centre to see *Swan Lake*. It had all been so unexpected, I told Miranda, having to be pleasant to them after having laughed at their little troll faces in church and stared at the black spots on the backs of their hands. And wondered about them always being together (and feared the same fate for us), always, always, even in the bathroom, we wondered, and did their hearts beat to exactly the same rhythm, did their hair grow the same length every day and would they die on the same day, thinking the same final thought? I told Miranda how Richard had handed me the note on the way home, "Count the adverbs." There had been more than two hundred, during a two-hour drive, and nearly all relating to the production. Remarkably, they had said, smoothly, superbly, unforgettably, tenderly, a host of veries and one very, very.

Miranda kissed me then and she held me, and I was comforted and rocked for a moment, as if I had been pulled from the sea onto a pod-shaped sampan, where the gentle lacing back and forth would secure me for a time. But only for a brief time, because we kissed again and then there was the sound of kissing, if nothing else, the sound of tongues reaching out, wet and quick like some intriguing form of sea life. Our hands, too, were moving here and there like the life of the coast will, sometimes as if by the buoyancy of water and sometimes as if by the force of will. I began to feel a part of that slippery and reflective life which exists at the borders of the sea, not certain if I were a creature of land or water, but always giving chase to one or the other element of desire, lifted along by that ecstasy which precedes the moment of knowing I must let go and be pulled off by the water's drag. And then it was . . . ah, ah, ah, those mysterious tugs of conclusion and burial which send the coastal creatures into the sand or further out to sea. At least that is how it seems to me now.

This morning I could not believe that I had slept through Miranda's awakening; I could not believe that I had slept at all. It is Saturday, but I remembered that she had told me she had to go into the city to see one of her few remaining students of English. Yesterday's clothing still lay on the floor and, maternally, I began to fold her pants and shirt, resisting the desire to breathe in her odour, but closing my window so that at least it would not be diluted by paint spray and the butchering of the market. Jocelyn and Willy then seemed to be rightfully mine—relations, sexual relations, I said to myself. I roused them from bed to take them out for breakfast, and, as I stepped into the busy street, I felt happily uncivilized.

I had possessed Miranda. I laughed at the fogies of the marketplace; ha, ha, ha, I thought of the crabs and misers who had pointed their stained, yellow fingers for her failure to pay, or her hat, or her boyfriends. I imagined myself laughing and laughing as I walked among them, as if I were the first human being to have been informed, radioed news that rendered all this repetitive and public activity a joke upon itself. Clowns. Toads of convention, I thought.

We left the congee stall and took our bowls down to a spot nearer the lifeguards' shack where we watched the waves roll in, each one landing today with a brave thump, as if aware of its sacrifice to the earth's indifferent and changing face. Willy had brought the soccer ball, which we kicked back and forth and into the water, getting ourselves soaked. Then abruptly, he took off to find some friend, which is like him, and Jocelyn and I rambled back home.

Elizabeth was sitting on the balcony when we arrived, smoking, her hair brushed on one side, and still matted from sleep on the other. I was feeling clever and undistracted. "Good morning," I said. "You're looking rather Janus-like today."

"Pardon me?" Elizabeth responded. She seemed a bit ill-tempered.

"You know, two-sided, two-dimensional, brushed and unbrushed."

"Oh yes. I didn't have the strength to finish before my cigarette. It's such a mess this morning."

"I'll brush it," I offered, an unlikely familiarity for Elizabeth and me, but I wanted to get my hands on someone else, as a chaser to my memories of Miranda, I guess.

To my amazement, Elizabeth said, "Go ahead," and I stood behind where she sat upon a crate, and began brushing.

"Don't you have anything to do?" Elizabeth asked Jocelyn, who had been standing, black-eyed and staring, as is her fashion.

"No," she replied, probably not fully understanding, but turning and running away, down the stairs in the one-two beat children will use when they have a plan laid.

That is when Elizabeth said, "There's a problem with Miranda."

"Oh," I said, leaning over her and looking closely at her face. "You have a little bit of sleep in the corner of your eye," but as I moved to dislodge it, Elizabeth pushed my hand away.

"What's going on with you?" she asked. "All this brushing and touching. You're making me feel a bit queasy."

"Nothing's going on," I said, straightening myself behind her, aware suddenly of a giddy bashfulness cradled among the bones of my pelvis. It reminded me of a bit of brownish, spoiled fruit. Then I began to laugh for what seemed to be a very physical reason, as if it must be so, as if all of the blood vessels in the remotest patches of my skin and inner organs were opening up so that I had to take gulping, seizing gasps of air to replenish the oxygen supply to my brain. I felt like Joel, and missed him for a moment, very much, although it was difficult to clasp on to any particular thought. I laughed again. I wanted to sail out from the balcony on breakable threads. I wanted to get away.

Impatiently, Elizabeth said, "Give me that brush."

I handed it over, but rather than continue with the brushing, she began talking, using the brush as an elocutionist might, waving it at me intermittently for emphasis.

"I was walking by the dentist's clinic yesterday morning," Elizabeth began, "and his receptionist came outside and actually hailed me into the office to show me Miranda's account. I'm not accustomed to this type of ignominy, you know. She owes five hundred and fifty dollars, Hong Kong. Apparently they have mailed her reminders, talked to her on the street, and now, as a last resort, they are asking me to intervene. I gave them one hundred dollars and they asked me to tell Miranda that she cannot make any further appointments until the account is paid."

Elizabeth turned on her crate to face me, and went on. "My question is, why would she not have their father tend to their teeth? It's the perversity of it that bothers me. Although that is certainly not all," she said, turning away again so that I could see only the back of her head as she spoke. "I have yet to receive any money for July and August's gas bills, or the three phone calls to Australia. And, who feeds the children most of the time? Who fed them this morning, for example?"

"I did," I said and repeated, "I did," feeling the need to confess twice.

Elizabeth smoked and watched the street, showing no signs of compassion whatsoever.

"She should have some money soon," I said.

"Yes, she should," Elizabeth shot back, stressing the word should. "I can agree with you on that. Just like she should develop some maternal instincts. They seem to have been eclipsed by some of her other instincts." There have been a few times in my life when I have, ever so briefly, fleetingly, hated Elizabeth. The last occasion was years ago in Calgary when she told me that ornamental horticulture was all part and parcel of the "social quackery" of the middle class. "What about function?" she asked me. "What about wheat?" and she handed me a calendar from the University of Alberta with all of the courses in crop science asterisked.

I handed it back to her saying, "No thank you, E. Actually, I am thinking of taking an evening course in topiary, you know, clipping shrubs into little deer or, who knows, maybe even ducks, little social quacks."

This time, though, my anger came steaming forth, unchecked. Moving around to face Elizabeth, I said, "You can be so boringly traditional." She had butted her cigarette and was in the process of standing and going inside, which she, of course, did not interrupt, leaving me to follow her backside into our dark and depressing hallway.

Undaunted, I said, "You have always been such a good little girl. Do you know what I mean? Despite all of this supposed unconventionality and disregard for fashion, your old clothes and your worn-out socialist dogma, you have always been the perfect little girl. The way you were in school, always ahead, always the most pleasing answers. I know what you were like. That time that short guy with the toupee, Professor Gunther, kept coming to see you. Richard and I were in first year and you were in your last year and you didn't even recognize the guy had a crush on you. Oh no, it was 'Oh, yes Professor Gunther, I do agree with you in part, but at the same time I would like to shock and amaze you with this genuinely original, yet well-founded thought.' Can't you stop being so . . . bloodless, just for a moment?"

Elizabeth was standing in the doorway to her room by this point, facing me at close range, and I continued shouting in this way, aware that nervous, white, gummy spit was beginning to form in the corners of my mouth.

"I don't think you've ever done a single thing in your life that was inappropriate," I added. "You seem to feel that it is your responsibility to sit back and critique us all, while at the same time luxuriating in the knowledge that you are beyond reproach. Beyond reproach," I repeated, aware of the muscles in my neck tightening.

Elizabeth, as I could have predicted, with a concerned yet dismissive expression, said, "I'm sorry if I offended you. I know you're fond of Miranda. I apologize. And now I have to shower and get going." And with that she squeezed by me and into the washroom.

This served to increase my rage, and as she showered, I stood outside the bathroom door and shouted, "Elizabeth! Elizabeth!"

"What?" she yelled back, irritated.

"I just want you to know that I am going to pay Miranda's dental bill. I'm going to do that right now," I said, trying to shout above the shower. "I'm going to pay the whole shot. And there won't be any politically correct receipt for it. I'll be rewarding negligence, that's what I'll be doing. And you hate that, don't you?"

"Yes, I do," screamed Elizabeth, which shocked and pleased me, and I said quietly to the bathroom door, "Oh, go to hell," then located my cheque book and went out.

I paid the dentist's bill. It was still morning and I was feeling refreshed and invigorated by my argument with Elizabeth, and aroused and almost euphoric from my night with Miranda, and, for the first time since my arrival here, the island became a confinement. Every direction I considered walking led to either a monastery or another village with yet another market place, a temple with its stale sacrifices, or worse, the dumb charity of the fields. I realized that there is not an inch of this island which has not been domesticated in some way, so well-used has it been.

Only the beach offered a bit of disorder, after I had walked a long way, past the restaurants to a trashy and fish-strewn little spit, where I looked for stones to throw and found very few. Miranda was inside of me then, like photosynthesis; I felt I could make new use of warmth and light, I could generate plans and action.

I could go home and look at the slides.

Elizabeth had intended to leave on the noon ferry, so she would be out of the way, I told myself, and so what if the children were home.

When I arrived, Jocelyn was standing in the hallway, playing with a Jacob's ladder, and Willy was still out. As for Miranda, there is no saying where she was. I set the slide projector on the table, facing it toward the balcony door, and with four purposeful slams, I closed the bedroom and bathroom doors, shutting off the light from their windows. Then, using only the light from the kitchen window, I plugged in the projector and plopped the slides into the carousel. Everything worked, as I knew it would. Charlie would not possess a faulty slide projector. Finally, I hung a towel over the kitchen window, securing it by hammering two nails into the soft and crumbly plaster. As I sat next to the projector, I thought to myself that I am certain God was no more pleased with the first production of light than I was with my darkness. It was close to utter.

With Jocelyn sitting next to me on a stool, I explained, "These are from a long time ago, when I was a little older than you are now."

The projector shone a lonesome spotlight on the balcony door and, even though it was cool in our hallway, I noticed that my hands were sticky, as if someone were planning to ask me to perform in that light, create shadow puppets or some other charade for a theatre of viewers. It was good that I had Jocelyn there with me, with her volumes of inarticulate childhood wisdom and her Jacob's ladder, falling and falling.

I knew what to expect; the seven scenes of clouds and the five of us, in the kitchen, that night. I had arranged them that way, even though the clouds had occurred after the kitchen scenes, chronologically.

The first image appeared, amazingly. It was the Formans' sugar bush and the sky above it, all fitting neatly upon the balcony door. "Those clouds are called cirrus, I think," I said to Jocelyn, pausing for a moment and moving on to the next two slides of the sky over Peg and Ken's farm, morning and night-time formations. These shots had had to do with folklore; I remembered Elizabeth speaking about red sky at night and red sky at morning, weather myths she had called them and had listed several, by means of hours of tedious stencilling, on a piece of yellow construction paper.

Next was a picture of our silo, with stratus clouds in the background. "Stratus," I said to Jocelyn, feeling that she should know a bit of weather terminology, "and now, cumulonimbus."

Jocelyn was unresponsive. The endless motion of the Jacob's ladder had a defiant quality to it, and I thought, if this were school, and I were a teacher, I would confiscate that thing. I began to worry that she knew her mother and I had slept together, although she gave no indication of such knowledge. The face of a child such as she is not accustomed to giving messages; the eyes simply lie in wait.

We watched a vista of sky with no earthly bearings whatsoever. "Clouds," I said.

"No special name?" Jocelyn inquired.

"Yes, but I don't know it."

The seventh and final cloud slide was of water and dark sky and had been taken at the foot of the cat-walk. I know because I was with Elizabeth the day that photo was taken. We had scrambled down that familiar, always damp and needle-covered pathway, late in February, long before the twenty-fourth of May, breaking the rule. I remember loving the cat-walk that day, for its whimsy, especially in spring – hidden roots which could trip and break necks or backs – and for its singleness of purpose, always bringing us to the water and, better yet, the secrets held by the water. I sat and looked at that picture for a long time, at those swells off in the distance, beyond the ice, experiencing a kind of charmed terror at the unstoppable motion of a wave.

Then we came to Richard, holding a stamp to the camera's eye. The colour was the way colour was back then, newly invented, more conspicuous, as if excited with its own pigmentation. Today's colours appear faded, by comparison. The brilliance of his red shirt made him seem albino, and in the background I was visible, at the fish pail, in jeans and a green sweater. How peculiar I began to feel at the sight of us all.

Next was Dad at the table, squinting through the magnifying glass at Elizabeth. We should have known, I guess; his plans must have been laid, behind that enlarged yet narrowed eye. We should have been able to see the clues beyond that glass.

"Who is that?" asked Jocelyn.

"That's my dad," I said, pushing the button to advance the carousel. "And that's my mother."

She was plugging in the kettle for tea, and for the steaming of stamps. Mom smiled in that generous and artless way she could, when Dad was happy.

Then we saw me, tipping the pail forward so that the fish could be photographed. There was the silver of the pail and a black arc in the water, a slippery and elusive bit of life, and my very pleased face.

It was very quiet and dark in our little theatre, but not dark enough. I suddenly became aware of light, what seemed to be a glaring strip of neon, coming from beneath the balcony door; I stopped it up with a rolled towel. I was reminded of being at a matinee, when the theatre door swings open and light of the afternoon washes in, so unforgivingly real, to shame us out of sentiment.

Then, click, I moved on to the last slide, of Dad and me, and the pail behind us. It was before he kissed me, just before, and he was looking down at me with, I guess it would be called a sidelong glance, as I faced the camera. That is all there was to the picture, along with a bit of steam above my shoulder, from the kettle.

"That's me," my lips said to Jocelyn, the way lips can at certain times, when public speaking must be done or when stopping to help at the scene of an accident.

Jocelyn stood and moved closer to look, and inspired by her, I did the same. The doorknob was positioned where a breast might have been, had I had any at the time, and Jocelyn, finding this amusing, grabbed the doorknob and turned it letting the door open a crack.

"Don't," I said.

She continued, laughing, and I shouted at her, "Leave it!"

I have never raised my voice to her before, and she took off down the stairs and outside, crying, which was just as well. I wanted to be alone.

The slide projector hummed stupidly. I stood to the side of the image on the balcony door, foolishly hoping to be able to catch a glimpse behind Dad's head, hoping for three dimensions instead of two. I touched him, his forehead, and then stood in front of the projection. We look so much alike now that I realized his features could be superimposed upon my own, his eyes upon mine, his mouth upon mine. I waited for something, a message, a bit of communion, but instead felt only ghoulish and ridiculous.

Turning off the projector lamp, I sat in the darkness for a while. That is when I thought the thought I have been putting off, the thought that is really a picture that comes only in brief flashes, moments of brilliance, much like the slides.

It happened that last night with Dad, after I had gone upstairs. I was in my room getting ready for bed, vaguely aware of Elizabeth and Dad talking downstairs. I remember a laugh and something about trigonometry. Dad asked Elizabeth if she wanted a ride home, and she said, "No, I'd rather walk. It's almost a full moon."

"You're sure now?" Dad asked.

And then there was a silence, a worrisome silence because it should not have been. There should have been a coat, and boots, maybe a hanger falling, but there was none of that and I wondered what was the matter. I knelt down by the old hot air grate to take a look.

It was necessary to get over to one side and put my cheek on the floor to achieve the best angle, and even then, the picture I saw was incomplete. There was the table, the stamps here and there and on the far side, Dad, his white shirt, his right arm around Elizabeth, and her, Elizabeth, holding on to Dad, her elbow, her jeans, their bodies held together in a queer and alarming way, their heads not visible; the angle was too short. Still, it's all too clear to me, and always will be, as if that image had been baked into my mind in Kodacolor.

I jumped into bed back then, knowing this was something I could not watch, and I pulled the blankets and pillows over my head. I closed my eyes and I pulled a blind down over that final picture of my father. I pulled it down and I have never really raised it since. Oh, I have peeked around of course, surmised what might be behind it, but never given it a good yank and sent it snapping up so that it's flung right off its supports.

I have got to talk to Elizabeth, I forced myself to think. It is time that it was done.

Sweat was dripping from my armpits when Jocelyn returned and I was flooded with warmth for her, for something else to think about, and for her mother. I apologized for shouting at her. We opened the doors and took down the towel from the kitchen window, allowing in the light and the life of the afternoon. I suggested that we go out to look for material to make some shelves for their bedroom, and that is what we did, with Willy's help. And now I am just putting in time, putting in time, until Miranda comes home, and the train jolts forward again.

Richard

It was the last day of August, a Friday night, and Richard had just prepared himself a fourth vodka martini with an olive. Customarily he drank, at the most, three martinis, but tonight there seemed indisputable evidence that Richard McDonagh became an improved person with alcohol. There is no doubt, he thought, I become more gregarious and loving, I want to compliment people or dance with them, I will listen to the most boring and self-endeared individuals. Or I will speak passionately on topics about which I know very little; the alcohol causes me to bubble forth with great wellsprings of wisdom. That evening, at the Blue Jay Variety, while paying for a jar of olives after his third drink, Richard had spoken at length with the storekeeper, Sangeet, a thin, clean-shaven man from New Delhi. There was a problem with vandalism in the neighbourhood.

"Oh, it is very bad," Sangeet had said, causing Richard to offer a sociology of wanton destruction.

"The kids are mad these days," he said. "They're mad about something," and he had listed several possible reasons for their anger. "Maybe it's too ugly in the city, maybe they don't do anything useful, maybe they're just stupid or reckless."

Sangeet had watched him with suspicion, as if all of his reasons were soft-headed. Richard, on the other hand, had begun to feel as if he could list reasons forever, reasons having to do with parents who had to work two jobs, maybe in casinos late at night, or who had short fuses and whacked their kids around too often. He had wanted to discuss all of these hypotheses, but Sangeet would have thought it out of character, or guessed that he was drunk, so Richard had paid for the olives and gone home.

"Maybe I should drink more often," Richard said to himself, sitting on his blue couch.

It was late, after midnight, and he was possessed with a kind of dervish of energy. He felt an attraction to the world – Reba, his squalid apartment and his box of clippings. Everything seemed to be giving off a hum, a quiet motor noise, like a refrigerator.

Looking through some clippings, Richard observed that their datelines were really somewhat poetic. "Rangoon, Santiago, Jakarta and Kinshasa," he read from his international pile, and from his Canadian section, "Pellmell Harbour," and "Maudsley." The Canadian clippings, being his favourites, tended to be almost entirely lined in yellow. Richard knew many of the victims' names and often muttered them to himself at his desk at work, or as he walked. Carolyn Applegate, for example. Carolyn had been on a foot bridge over a chasm in a provincial park when she died. It had given way and she had fallen, no doubt as in a dream, marvelling at the desperate certainty of falling downward, through air. Gerald Kastendieck was another name. He had been shot by a hunter and that was all there was to that.

Richard not only dwelt upon the victims, but also their families. He imagined talking with them; he considered them all to be a community of the inexplicably and untimely bereaved.

As he sat upon the couch, martini glass resting on his right knee, Richard concentrated on the lives of Carolyn Applegate and Gerald Kastendieck with the intensity it is said is required for an act of telepathy. He wanted to roll back the days so that he could warn them both, bound out of the woods waving both arms above his head. Richard asked himself why a person would not have some prescience regarding an event as large as one's own death, if not bulletins in the mind saying, "Stop! Go no further!" then at the very least, a foreboding sensation. How can there not be some inkling, he thought, when we know so much of what will happen, the most likely words our friends will speak when we are met at the airport, the way in which our muscles will tire if we sit in a certain chair, where the traffic will bottleneck in the mornings and what our supervisors at work will be thinking on an hourly basis. "It doesn't seem right," Richard said out loud. "There must be some warning too subtle for the human brain to appreciate."

Richard's intoxicated sympathy for everything around him gave way then to a compulsion, a plan he had made several times in recent weeks but had rejected for its anarchistic motives. Now, however, he knew that he would go ahead and do something he probably should not; he would telephone unknown relatives of the dead. And then, to compound the situation, he would concoct lies.

It was not an impetuous decision, this. He had chosen the Pellmell Harbour and Maudsley clippings long ago because he knew that they must be villages or small towns (and the tiny black dots in his atlas had, of course, confirmed this). With the Kastendieck and Applegate surnames it had been easy to obtain numbers from the information operator, although there were two Applegates in Pellmell Harbour, preventing a completely linear arrangement of possible events. He would call both if he had to.

Richard handled several of the clippings for a while, lifting each one and setting it down in a quick and diffident manner, as if about to present a talk to a group of scholars, a presentation of research that had been so complex, and tied together so many unlikely fragments of information, that if he did not begin at once the tentative map of significance he had created might tear apart. There was a feeling of great activity within Richard's chest, the vibration that might be received standing amid the old-fashioned style of secretarial pool, with twenty or more typists working at great and clattering speeds.

"I'm heading for something a little bit crazy," he thought, placing the phone on his lap and rolling upon his chair to the wall jack. "Perhaps telephones should only be rented to those who have proven themselves in some way, those who have passed a licensing procedure and have demonstrated that they can be trusted with the companionable dial tone."

"However," Richard spoke to Reba, "there is a logic to what I am doing. There is a sort of freemasonry which exists among those of us whose relatives' disappearance, or demise, or misfortune, has been written up in the press."

He held the Kastendieck number, the special arrangement of digits; the operator had given him permission to break and enter, in a far-off way. Her voice had been so sleepy and friendly on the night she had given Richard the number, that she had sounded like a spouse who had just been awakened, and Richard had wanted to talk for a while. But, before he had had an opportunity to ask her about the weather in British Columbia, she had disconnected herself.

It was late for phone calls, even to B.C., but Richard had no compunctions; it was the drink. He knew enough to carry on an informed conversation; he knew that Gerald Kastendieck had been a fourth year biology student at Simon Fraser University, and that he had been at his parents' home for the summer, working for the fish and wildlife people. That was enough. Richard dialled the one and the area code and the seven numbers, pausing after the third one as he always did, leaving a place for the dash.

The ringing began. Richard wondered what on earth type of dwelling the telephone called into. After the sixth ring there came a hello. The voice was male and hopeful.

"Hello," said Richard. "I hope I'm not calling at a really bad time. I'm in Hong Kong and I've lost track of the time difference between here and there. Richard McDonagh's my name; I was a friend of Gerald's."

"You knew Gerry? Where did you say you were calling from?"

"Hong Kong. I just read the piece in a Canadian paper while I was at the library today. I'm very sorry."

Richard no longer believed that he was lying. He had known Gerald Kastendieck, he said to himself, and he had liked him very much.

"How did you know Gerry?" the voice asked.

"School. We were in school together, same major. I'm over here for my last year on an exchange programme."

"You must be an ace student too, then, like Gerry was."

"Oh, it's not as great as it sounds."

There was a silence. Richard could tell that this was a man who believed it was necessary to be cheerful; disappointment and sorrow were not considered to be part of his entitlement.

"You know how crazy Gerry was about wildlife," Mr. Kastendieck said. "He always was, even when he was three years old he had ducks and frogs. It was like a zoo here. Well, now the Optimist Club here has put up a scholarship in his name, for a deserving biology student."

"Well, that's something to be proud of," Richard said, and then added, with a kind of welled-up fanatacism, "It's too bad. It doesn't make a lot of sense, does it?"

With this question, Richard felt the type of ignoble gratification a mad person might, after having waited days or weeks to achieve the perfect circumstance for his ardent and inadvisable commentary. He wondered if he had said something disgraceful. But the response from Mr. Kastendieck was even and pleasant.

"It was good of you to call, Richard. And don't worry about the time. I kind of listen for the phone late at night. I'm a cabinet maker and there's one crazy contractor who phones sometimes at three in the morning. That's who I thought you were."

Richard pictured a smallish man with a mustache, examining his own cupboards, opening a drawer and closing it again, slowly, as if it held a collection of miniature, standing figurines.

"Is it busy in Hong Kong?" Mr. Kastendieck asked. "Lots of construction?"

"They seem to be expanding the transit system," Richard answered. "Lots of noise and dust."

"Not much going on here," said the voice from Maudsley. "Like I said, I thought you might be crazy Neil with a job."

"I'm sure things will pick up. Anyway, I wanted to extend my sympathy, and now I should let you get some sleep."

"OK then. Thanks for calling, Richard. I appreciate it."

After hanging up, Richard felt a little like a vandal, a decently dressed and reasonably paid vandal, who had thrown a load of heavy and jagged garbage into a stand of darkly swaying water plants.

"Maybe I should let Pellmell Harbour sleep," Richard said to Reba. But he could not stop himself. He was driven by a fossil fuel kind of energy, soon to be exhausted, he feared.

It would be five in the morning there. Richard dialled the M.K. Applegate number and a female voice answered brightly, which helped Richard to authenticate his greeting. "Hello, Mrs. Applegate," he said. "I know I'm calling at a ridiculous hour and that you don't know me, but my name is Richard McDonagh and I was an acquaintance of Carolyn's."

"Oh," Mrs. Applegate said, "it was a terrible thing, wasn't it? And it took so long with the provincial park, the officials and so on, determining liability and so on. Dan and Tess had a terrible time."

"Dan and Tess?" Richard inquired.

"You know, Carolyn's parents. This is her grandmother you're talking to. Dan and Tess have had so much to put up with and that includes me. Yesterday, I lost my grocery cart at the A & P. I get confused – that's the word they all use. Why a young person like Carolyn would go while I'm still here with my pills and dahlia roots, I'll never know."

Richard immediately warmed up to Mrs. Applegate. He took a very big sip of his martini and was about to comment sympathetically regarding Carolyn, but Mrs. Applegate continued on. "I took zinc for a while but it did no good as far as I can see. Now it's devil's claw I have. That boy of, oh, what's their names, who are they? It doesn't matter. He knows all about herbs and so on, lived with the Indians for a while. He told me to take devil's claw. I said, sure, as long as it doesn't turn me into one of Satan's choice."

She laughed a hearty, well-used laugh, the sort of laugh that would earn both friends and enemies at the Women's Institute, or any place where a roll was called and decorum prevailed.

"What's your name again?" Mrs. Applegate asked.

"McDonagh."

"Where are you from again? There are some McDonaghs down in Lanyard Bay. You're not part of that crowd are you?"

"I'm living in Calgary, actually."

"Calgary! Say, you're clever out there in the west. Tell me, what is it that would make a brain stop working? I took the zinc and now this devil's claw and nothing seems to help."

Richard said, "I can't say, Mrs. Applegate. I work in a library and sometimes I read in reference material about the brain. They say large parts of it do nothing at all, so, that's the way it is for everyone. Maybe if all of the parts of our brains were working we'd know better than to drive on certain days, or what bridges not to cross. We'd be able to see into the future and make sense of the past."

"Sense!" Mrs. Applegate hooted scornfully. "There's no sense. That's why I have begun attending the Pellmell Anglican Church. I'm waiting for them to put things in order for me before I go, and it's a big job, too. Sometimes I get a good old laugh out of it. I told Dan and Tess I thought I might join the Glory Tabernacle. They talk gibberish, you know. I'd fit right in. They might even take me for a prophet." Then she laughed again.

By this time Richard did not wish to remind Mrs. Applegate why he had called, so he told her he really had to go and that it had been a pleasure talking with her.

"Well, likewise, I'm sure," came the reply, and they both hung up. Richard unplugged the telephone and replaced it on the refrigerator where it sat, crustacean-like, seeming to be breathing beneath its shell. He rolled this way and that in his kitchen, feeling resolutely awake, capable of writing an exam or doing memory work if called upon. Answers to crossword puzzle clues would have come instantly to mind, if Richard had had the desire to undertake one.

"It's so late," he said to himself, "and I have been making phone calls, phone calls which could be described as both morbid and fanciful and which would suggest to me that I am more fucked than ever. And now here I sit, alone and for some reason, woebegone." The fact that he would never meet the wifely telephone operator, or the Kastendiecks, or Mrs. Applegate, had caused a sudden and quick rotation within him, a turning toward the overwhelming awareness of all that can never be known, all that is shown to us briefly, then whisked away, leaving only a name or a photograph or a telephone number.

"I need information. It's information that I actually need," Richard announced loudly, leaving his martini glass on the kitchen table and rolling into the living room. There was an article he wanted, an article copied from *The Atlantic Monthly*, on the likelihood of contacting intelligence elsewhere in the universe. There were formulae and numbers, large and breathtaking numbers, numbers to the power of thousands and millions. Richard located it and flopped into bed. The yellow highlighted passages seemed too bright, but he began to read.

The chances of communicating with another civilization were

remote, the author said. The light years of distance alone made the idea almost unworkable. And anyway, there was probably no one else out there. Using a formula known as the Drake equation, one scientist had computed an estimate of only one civilization in the universe: ours. Planetary life was the result of grand and improbable coincidences. Communication with another such set of coincidences was unlikely to the power of kerjillions. And then, the author asked, if we did contact another form of life, what would we want to know? The technological? The genetic wizardry? The smallest units of matter? And to what use would we put this?

Richard changed positions in bed, stretched out flat on his back and read some more. Life comes and goes, perhaps, the author said, with the ability to communicate bringing with it the ability to self-destruct. Just as we are at the point of reaching another globe, just as the very unlikeliest is about to occur, one or the other goes poof. The universe is a place, the scientist claimed, where every few eons a lonely call for companionship rambles out of existence, never heard.

Richard dropped the article on the floor. "Oh, what does this guy know?" Richard asked himself. "What does he know of Mrs. Applegate or Mr. Kastendieck and me? My lonely call for companionship didn't ramble out of existence unheard. They heard," Richard said to Reba, hiccuping with such sudden force his chest ached. "They answered my questions, more or less."

And no, he had not wanted the technological details. What type of gun? How old the bridge? What he had wanted were those small units though, yes, he had wanted those. The little bits of Mr. Kastendieck's and Mrs. Applegate's hearts, the smallest units of matter, the tiniest bits of disorder, so that they could be bound together with his. Put them all together in a petrie dish, all our units of bad luck, create a little culture, Richard thought. Keep it warm, grow something new, some type of sweepstake with an erotic and promising smell. People will come from other galaxies just to sniff at it.

And at that, Richard's wakefulness left him. He fell heavily asleep and dreamed of the infinite space filled with wavering signals, indigenous radio waves and random chirping static, which everyone seemed to understand.

Gayle

It is Sunday morning and I have been up since before the sun, sitting and watching the village awaken. Everything looks slightly different to me now, although how I am not exactly sure yet. There is a peacefulness I am aware of, knowing that the others are asleep, and a dispassion in my own wakefulness. I will begin with Miranda.

Immediately after our night together, she began to arrange events so that she was rarely at home. Suddenly she had a fulltime job at the travel agency, so that in the mornings she was up and gone to mass, and then the ferry, and in the evenings not home until seven, by which time I had fed Jocelyn and Willy.

I was not resentful about this. Oh no, not me, all puffed up with suspense as I was, like a wind sock, blowing this way and that in response to Miranda's every word and gesture. Once she arrived home, Miranda would putter here and there and eventually enter her room to meditate, and I would walk by to glance in or stand for a moment, envious of her silly mantra and a little disdainful of the way in which she always slumped forward as she meditated. After about half an hour of this, during which time Jocelyn may have come inside once or twice to show me a stone from the beach or put some private treasure into her bathroom bag, Miranda would arise and go to her loom and begin to weave. It seems the headaches have ceased to be a concern. I would then bring her tea and sit upon the crates and pillows which serve as our couch and wait for a signal from her, a lifting away of the heavy curtain between us. But it did not happen and I could not ask for it to happen, could not bring myself to question her because I could not forfeit the waiting on the couch, could not deny myself the elated prognostications taken from Miranda's remote face. I am a fool in this regard.

She would weave and weave and the walking figures would take form. Each motion of the shuttle was, I knew, a measurement, a clocking of the distance between us. The neighbour man could be heard piling bags on to a trolley, while I might have felt an irritation with anyone who would buy such bright and gaudy items. That is how it went.

Then the children would return from outside, and Miranda became the attentive mother. She would read to them and they would fall asleep, and without saying good-night, so would Miranda.

There were no evening walks. I sat in my room staring at the eleven stamps that have begun to peel off the wall, and imagined screaming at Miranda, or strangling her. One night I unravelled the entire camera strap she gave me and left it in a pile of worm-like threads beneath my bed.

I do not give up easily in these matters, though. Eventually, as the night wore on, I lay there hoping that she would join me or wondering if I should join her. So much tension was being dispersed from my bedroom that I believe it must have filled the hallway, that the walls were sweating from the intensity of it and that the naked light bulb, left on for Elizabeth, shone more brightly on those evenings, as if searching.

Elizabeth would at last come home and turn the light off, and at that time I could tell myself, "The day is over." But it was not really, not until Miranda had left the following morning, and I, awake and listening, could relax and renew my optimism, inventing rambling and delusional explanations for Miranda's behaviour.

This went on for five days, exactly as I am telling it. I did some work each day for Charlie, Jocelyn might have brought me a flower or Willy asked for money, but as for the rest, it was as if we were following a schedule designed to drive me mad – the meditation, the slumping forward, the weaving, the silence, the mothering, the sleeping.

Then on Friday evening she asked me to join her on the beach.

"I'll grab my chair," I said, wanting to take action, feeling an almost manly preparedness.

"I don't think I'll bother with mine."

"Then I'll bring the tatami mat."

I had to bring something, I had to be carrying something in my arms.

It was a beautiful evening, with a tour junk out in the bay and the distant voices of English-speaking people, and here and there a sampan fish-tailing. The lifeguards were gone and a British woman I know of, Lydia Toynbee, sat alone in the one Chinese restaurant at the water's edge, wearing a black hat and gloves and reading, a pitcher of beer in front of her. In general, the expatriates here seem to drink too much.

I spread the tatami mat and sat, inviting Miranda to join me, but, "No," she said, "I think I'll stand." She had something to say.

"Yes, OK, say it," I said. I was unsure as to how to arrange my face, what expression would best ready me.

"It's about what happened between us," Miranda began, standing above me like a pale plant, swaying, long-stemmed, etiolated from too little light. "It was a mistake, I realize now. It's just not for me, with women. Although that's not all of it. It's more that I think I should draw a halt to my activity for a while. There's a limit, after all. Maybe that's what I've discovered with you. That there's a limit, after all. That's what my mother used to say to me, 'There is a limit, Miranda.' I guess she was right."

There was a bark of laughter from the party junk. I looked around and saw that Lydia Toynbee had ordered another pitcher of beer. Edward Hopper might have wanted to paint her, I thought.

"I've been talking with Gordon," Miranda said. "We're trying to work something out. It won't be easy – we've been apart for more than two years—but we're both more ready now. More ready, more committed, more resigned; I'm not sure which is the most appropriate term. We're prepared for a long journey together, it seems. I'm relieved, really. However, I'm sure it all sounds quite boring to you, Gayle."

"No, not at all."

She had stopped swaying.

"Sit down with me now," I said, but she would not.

"I have to get back to the kids."

She was sorry, I could see that she was sorry, but she walked away nonetheless, and the feeling, watching her disappear along the beach, was of two long, narrow taproots being extracted from the soles of my feet. She would return to the apartment, I thought, where she would repeat yesterday's actions, walk here and there with towels and pyjamas and conduct the children's prayers. In their dark room she would look like a white watch face against a brown arm.

Tick, tock, tick and I will be gone; I knew it then.

I sat on the mat. Fluids sloshed within me; I could hear them, I could feel them when I squeezed my wrist. We are not much different from the ocean, I thought. Chemistry is a sneaky devil which tricks us into believing otherwise.

I sat for some time. Lydia Toynbee closed her book and walked off along the dark road to her home, two miles toward Pui O. She carried her flashlight, as is her custom.

The junk came closer and I could hear talk, loud laughter about chicken feet and what is sold in the market in Canton. "Revolting," someone said. I hated them all intensely.

The thought of sitting there all night, or of lying down in the lifeguards' shelter, appealed to me. Either option was much more attractive than the image of the light bulb burning in the hallway and Miranda's self sleeping in the adjacent room, with none of its life wanting to be a part of mine. The finality of it made me a little woozy and incredulous, the way I had felt after seeing the amazing fat lady at the Ex. in Toronto. And yet, what had I expected? I must answer that, as I sort through the three months' worth of possessions I have to pack or send to Canada.

Charlie's house seemed like the place to be, so I rolled up the tatami mat and plunged into the dark woods between the two stones where the high path begins. I must have tripped over a dozen roots and stones, and each time I said out loud, "It's OK, no harm done." I was like a drunk.

At the rich man's house the lights were on. I thought of peeking inside again, and sneaked up to the same window the three of us had looked through weeks ago. A cat padded over and looked up at me, paws on the window ledge, and in the other room, the kitchen, were the voices of a man and a woman, the artist girlfriend, no doubt, and the businessman. Although they were speaking in Cantonese, I thought, "These are the sounds of people who love one another."

My behaviour was not at all furtive; on the contrary, I felt I belonged with them, so walked down into their garden where Miranda and I had drawn one another. There was no sound, only the moon and trees. I thought that if there were a way in which I could untether myself from the snare of events and stay right there, embedded in that moment, I would have. That is when I recognized that sorrow was tagging me like some small night animal, a dark and vanishing life, caught only by the peripheral vision.

The path downhill to Charlie's was better lit because of the moon and the lack of foliage, and I hurried along without tripping once. It was midnight when I arrived and Pui Sin had gone to bed, but Charlie was up, as I had anticipated. The entire story of Miranda and me came out, which before the telling I had imagined would take hours to relate but, in fact, took less than ten sentences; it was really a mathematically tidy group of thoughts. Finite. But with that infinity of any number of possible outcomes fractioned between each pair. And that is what brought the tears on. "I actually think I love her," I said.

"I know you do," Charlie said as he made tea and told me about a woman he had loved in Shanghai. She had left him for a banker. "The stereotype, too," Charlie went on, "overweight, fleshy lips, a seeming patina of grease on his fingers." Thinking for a moment, Charlie added, "Although it really is not accurate to say that she left me. She was never really with me, to begin with. Hope was her name—isn't that poetic?—Hope Lillow. I presented myself as an option which she did not select. It had nothing to do with the genuineness of my love. Mr. Mutual Funds or whatever his name was, was her preference. You'll get over it. I did. Life is a teacher, you know, with a big desk full of realities and we students sit at our little desks filled with illusions. Almost every day we make a swap with the teacher."

Then, with great excitement, Charlie changed the subject.

"They're planning a big demonstration in town tomorrow," he began. "Ten thousand out possibly, to see the Foreign Secretary off. Britain's going to abandon these people. I've been saying so all along. They can go on ad nauseam about commitment but there won't be any U.K. citizenship for these people."

It was good to be with Charlie in his house, good to have an issue to dwell upon. So the people were angry. Good, I thought, good.

Charlie cleared off the bed in the spare room for me, and when I mentioned that I wanted to be up early and off to Hong Kong, he began a shopping list and dug out a library book to be returned. I fell asleep and woke up with not a thought between the two occasions. What a gift the night is, stopping us and throwing us to the ground as it does. In the early grey, I was up before either Pui Sin or Charlie, showered in their outdoor bath house and hurried off on the flat route, as we call it, along the valley floor, past the rice and chicken coops toward the ferry terminal. I wanted to make the earliest sailing, the one before Miranda.

There is sleep and there is movement; these are the two essentials, at least that is what I believed yesterday morning. Even the plants seemed to move very quickly as I jogged along, disappearing behind my visual field as if I were on wheels. The greenery on either side reminded me of driving the concession roads outside Unity with Dad. The green would fall away outside the truck in the same blurring way, the maples and milkweed and burdocks all overlapping, creating an illusion of speed and a feeling that arrival might never be necessary.

I ran faster on the boardwalk, through farms, past aging brick buildings, past dogs in cages, past one old woman with buckets suspended from a bamboo rod, past laundry, to the edge of the village. Not even my favourite restaurant was open for coffee yet, so I went straight to the ferry to drink the horrid Nescafe, relieved that I had arrived in time for the seven o'clock sailing.

It was the usual mothers and children with baskets, and men with bicycles and newspapers and playing cards on the lower deck. I did not sit, but circulated until I located a spot close to a huge, slopping barrel of cuttlefish. They were dead and their suckers rocked in the brine peacefully; even in death the life of the sea carries on. I understood at that moment why a person would be content to be buried at sea, borne away, made light by the strength and the heaviness of water.

As I stared into the barrel of fish, the resolve to ask Elizabeth about that last evening with Dad, about what I saw from my bedroom, entered and filled me the way a drug in the bloodstream will, a slow process, so slow it is only noticed afterward when the person says, "I was not like this fifteen minutes ago. Half an hour ago I was not aware of anything at all. My mind was sitting in my skull with no particular effect and now my senses feel as if they might belong to someone else, as if they had been borrowed for a while, from a stranger with a different set of plans."

Everything seemed provisional and tipsy then, like the boat. The others, the men and women, all appeared to be so comfortable, as if each place where they sat or stood had been carved to fit the soles of their feet or the dimensions of their behinds, whereas I was unable to find even a level piece of flooring near the fish barrel. So misplaced did I feel by my own thoughts that I went to the bathroom to look in the mirror for reassurance. There I was. This strangeness or stranger had obviously entered via my pores or my lungs, like a gas, had compressed itself into my capillaries, maybe, but I decided that I could accommodate it. It could ride along with me.

Pacing the deck and watching the city skyline approach, I imagined Miranda, in one half hour's time, viewing the same scene, and seven hours later, Elizabeth also. By half-past three, Elizabeth would be climbing the steps of the British Council Building and that is where I planned to intercept her, in less than eight hours' time. No changing that fact, I thought. No way to slow down the rotation of the earth, no way to mount it like some Amazonian charioteer and rein it in.

We docked, and because of the heaviness of Charlie's book, Volume One of the *Dictionary of the History of Ideas*, I struck off first for the library, walking. The university was, as always, an asylum from the tumult of the city; a person expects to see classes of lady students identifying birds or arranging flowers, so turn-of-the-century and impractical is it, in the midst of all this business and trade.

After returning the book, I walked the grounds, past the banyan tree which caused my face to redden a little with its arms and fruit and its secret insects, and I hurried on, attempting not to think of Miranda. The gardeners were digging beds nearby and one of the fellows I have talked to before stopped to tell me what they were trying to accomplish. I listened and pretended to understand, wanting to go and wanting to stay. I was feeling both constrained and hurried by my plan to see Elizabeth, as if participating in a three-legged race with myself as partner, always pulling ahead by a fraction of a beat.

Back on the sidewalk, heading into Central, I coached myself on what I should ask of Elizabeth. It was reminiscent of the time I finally decided to talk to Mom, had myself all prepared, coming home from university with some notes and a little bit of hash. I remembered that I had intended to ask her to analyze Dad's behaviour within a political context: the cultural materialist's etiology of depression and other mental states. I knew she could do it; I knew she would have done it, if I had not put it off and put it off, until she had her heart attack and died on us.

I tried to condense what I wanted to ask of Elizabeth into one question. One question, only. "You could say . . . what?" I said to myself. "Exactly what was going on between you and Duncan McDonagh, before he disappeared. No, too much of an accusation. Did you and Duncan simply like each other a lot or . . . ? No. Better to make it an essay type question, the sort historians like. The events of the evening of December 4, 1968, at the McDonagh home near Unity, Ontario, were a prelude to, no, sequel to, no, part of a larger scenario, central to which were the personality of Duncan McDonagh and his relationship to you. Please comment."

"You should write that down," I said to myself, and "good idea."

I was walking very quickly as I thought; the glass buildings were so bright in the early morning sun that they seemed to waver like candlelight in my eyes. I focussed on the black and lumpy squatters' shacks off to the north and began wondering if Miranda and the kids would move in there if they could not make it with Gordon. I imagined Miranda, with her disregard of the environment, making a squalid home for the three of them, Willy joining a gang, hiding knives beneath wads of bedding, and Jocelyn's eyes becoming darker and more sunken. She would fill her bag with the paraphernalia of a fearful existence, a few tampons to examine from her mother's supply, a picture from a magazine of accident victims bleeding, pamphlets taken from the clinic on AIDS and other sexually transmitted diseases, Band-Aids and toilet paper, of course, and muscle relaxants stolen from the drugstore, to have on hand for her mother. I worry that they won't get by without me.

Down in Central, I wove my way through the narrow streets, past noodle vendors and piles of eggplant which looked somewhat sinister, so purplish-black and stretched. The China Department Store was a welcome change with its neatly stacked shelves of packages, white and red. It is like walking among beds of carnations in certain quarters of that store. The aisles are very wide and the several fans create an outdoor atmosphere.

Charlie wanted Running Pony shampoo and four tablets of the White Geranium lined writing paper he uses. After locating these items I stood by the long, glass pharmacy counter studying the powders and creams in their mysterious containers. There was a pyramidal pile of little triangular cases, metal, with no markings whatsoever. I asked the clerk what they were and he answered, looking at me slyly, "For love, for make love." Then, smiling confidently, he added, "He not love, you give this, a secret . . . he love you."

"I'll take one," I said, paid the twenty-four Hong Kong dollars and slipped it into my bag. I was in the mood for a remedy.

Outside I wandered aimlessly, thinking of Elizabeth. She would be up, I realized, and her day's journey would have begun. For each step I took, she would also take a step, and no matter what the direction, our paths would cross and we would have to divvy up the responsibility for Duncan McDonagh in a different way.

I went left, then right, then left again, and looking up, saw the sign for the Sunning House Hotel. I believe now that I must have been chauffeured there by some remote and libidinous part of my brain; Joel would have been able to name the lobe and would have delighted in describing its grey, endocrine will. I decided to go inside the Sunning House; it seemed an unexpected gift that this option even existed, that I could walk through the lobby, at least, only to see it, only to know where Miranda and Maurice had kept their afternoon assignations.

The Sunning House Hotel is a low building, only three stories, and made of yellow brick. I stood on the steps for a while, watching families come and go with suitcases, and young couples, and the occasional businessman; it was an opportunity to imagine Maurice and Miranda climbing the stairs and going through the conventions of checking in, signing the register and requesting room thirty-three.

The lobby did indeed have the same tile flooring as the island rich man's house, as Miranda had said. Behind the desk was a clerk whose hair feathered with each oscillation of the fan sitting upon the counter. I had not really planned to say what I said, I had not planned anything at all; it was the grey, endocrine will again, I suppose. "I'd like to have a look at one of your rooms," I said, "something on the third floor preferably. Is thirty-three empty? I've heard it's lovely," I added and laughed inwardly.

Without speaking, the desk clerk handed me the key. His indifference thrilled me.

There was no elevator. The stairwell and hallway seemed to contain all of the sad, stale odours of departure – tobacco, cleaning fluids, overcoats, shoe polish, perfumed hair. There was not a sound, only the idiotic beating of my wayward heart. What exactly was I doing? I wondered.

Room thirty-three was too sparsely decorated to be called unattractive. There were only a bureau, a chair, an end table supporting a green travesty of a telephone, and the bed. Yes, the bed. I could not avoid the bed, could not avoid that burden of intimacy which comes from imagining a lover with someone else.

Remembering that Miranda had willed away her attachment to Maurice in the bathroom, I decided that that was where I wanted to go. Perhaps I could do the same. The door was swollen, just as Miranda had described it, and it scraped against the linoleum as I entered, squeezing myself between the door and sink. Something about the closeness of the room, the bed beyond the door, the shrouded eroticism of hotel rooms, and the thought of Miranda – the willing away of which was hopeless – hit me in the way humidity will when stepping outside of an air-conditioned building. The memory of her settled first in my lungs and moved from there over my skin and inside of me, and I became enlarged, as if I were filling every corner of that tiny room with my urgent need, so that it took only five or six strokes of my finger to come, jerking everything back to a size that could be contained. I splashed water on my face, then yanked on the peeling bathroom door with such force the linoleum tore.

Sitting on the edge of the carefully made bed, I watched the telephone for a while, the green telephone, thinking that I would like to call Miranda, wherever she might be. I realized that I had never once spoken to her on the phone. But when I picked up the receiver, there was nothing, no dial tone, just the weight of the unresponsive plastic, like a toy in my hand. The entire room began to give off a feeling then of imaginary life. I walked out and returned the key to the desk clerk, who did not even look up when I said thank you.

There followed more walking. I was like a person on a leash; someone else seemed to be laying plans for me. "How about the Mandarin Hotel for lunch?" this someone suggested and I said, "Certainly, why not?" I had been there before and I liked the woman who worked as a towel attendant in the washroom; May, her name tag read.

Once there, I went immediately to see May, to show her my container of aphrodisiac. She held it, opened it, sniffed the yellow powder and nodded approvingly. "*Ho-hoah,*" she said, meaning it's good, it will have the desired effect. She seemed to be familiar with the substance, so I asked what it was made of and in answer to my question she positioned her two index fingers on her forehead, like devil's horns. "Antlers?" I asked, and she continued to point her fingers at me, then laughed and poked my shoulder and laughed again. She was still giggling when I left, wondering what animal had sacrificed a prong or possibly a life for my sake. It did not concern me, however. Very little yesterday invoked the name of nature; I was too busy scurrying in pursuit of that which travels at a speed greater than mere survival.

In the dining room I sat myself down with tea and studied my container of love-dust, smelling its musty animal scent and tasting its bone flavour. Would Miranda notice it, I wondered, stirred into her dried bean curd soup?

I thought about Joel and what he would have had to say. I knew exactly what he would have said in that situation. He would have said, "Why don't you take it, Gayle? Why contemplate giving it to Miranda? She's not the one who suffers from love-truncation. You think you would care about her six months from now if she reciprocated? Ha!"

I heard Joel say Ha! as clearly as if he were sitting across the table from me. "Try it," I heard him say. "It might free up a few neurotransmitters which have been trapped somewhere, stuck in a synapse for decades. It might reactivate a sleeping portion of your cortex or awaken a vestigial horn of love, deep in your brainstem."

Laughing a little at how well I could imagine Joel's comments, then feeling a bit angry with him, I dumped the powder into my tea and stirred. The colour turned to a milky shade of dishwater but I drank it in four gulps, then refilled my cup and began a bemused anticipation of change: the ability to love in a deep, enduring and correct manner, a Confucian way, gentlewomanly and wisely, to love for long periods of time and without flight.

Nothing immediately occurred. I ate chicken and peppers and tofu with bean sauce, then went outside.

People were collecting with signs and banners, hurrying downhill as if the wind might up-end them. My first thought was that the powder I had drunk was hallucinogenic and that a day of completely out-of-context visions awaited me, riotous demonstrations, followed by fields of corn and perhaps warships in the harbour, firing upon the island of Peng Chau. But the people seemed very genuine. Their banners were in Chinese and English and read, "British Betrayal" and "Justice Now" and "Shame, Britain, Shame."

It was a banner reading "We can't Waite any longer!" that reminded me of the British Foreign Secretary Andrew Waite's visit. He was leaving after three days of speeches in which the people of Hong Kong had been told to expect nothing of Britain when the lease runs out. Hundreds of people were heading to Kowloon to line Nathan Road as Mr. Waite was driven to the airport. I fell in with a group of very young, very angry people, and boarded the Star Ferry with them. They inquired if I were British and when I said "No, Canadian," I was granted acceptability.

By that time I no longer felt as if I were attached to one particular leash; there were several. I was moving with the forces of history, theirs, mine, the aphrodisiacal chemicals in my bloodstream, and the South China Sea beneath the ferry. People were wearing yellow, for betrayal I was told, except for me in Elizabeth's green jumper. So packed together were we that it was like a field of rape being rafted over to the mainland and for a moment I missed Richard and Joel, just being at home, so intensely, with such a voiding of my strength, that I felt my limbs might fall from my torso and I would be trampled underfoot.

I held together though, and travelled along with the demonstrators to Nathan Road where I found a spot to stand. People were very unhappy with Mr. Waite's speech of the night before; only if things went catastrophically wrong in China would Britain think of opening its doors to the Hong Kong Chinese, he had said.

I was with the people and I was not, because by then I could no longer disregard the sight of the British Council Building, off to my left, looming and so upright. Nevertheless, I stood and waited and shouted when Sir Andrew passed by; then, with equal interest, watched the yellow shirts fill the street and return to the ferry, leaving in their wake Kowloon, as always, moving and warm and exploding with goods.

There was a bar I knew of, from Miranda, a seedy little place right on Nathan Road called the Mai Tai, where I decided I should have a drink. The powdered horn had had no effect on any of my faculties as far as I could tell and I needed something to promote the organization of my unsteady thoughts.

The interior of the Mai Tai was dark. High-backed, red vinyl-covered booths filled the place, their colour in the gloom being that of clotted blood. I felt as if I were scooting along one of Lennart Nilsson's arterial passages as I slid into the booth.

A group of men stood at the bar, sailors I guessed, and another man, pimpish in appearance, stood apart from them. I wondered where Miranda liked to sit in the Mai Tai and what it was that brought her to that place. Pills maybe, I surmised, her so-called nerve pills. It caused me pain to think of her associating with that fellow at the bar in his long cuffs and his white shoes and his knowledge of all that is for sale in this place giving him an eager fluorescence. I hoped that he had never touched Miranda.

The waitress brought me a scotch and a round, scalloped paper coaster which I filled with notes. I pencilled out my thoughts for Elizabeth which I no longer have with me, but can remember. This is what I wrote: "Elizabeth, Elizabeth – Tell me what went on. For years I have been afraid to ask because I didn't want to know. You know more than I do – I know you do because I saw the two of you that night doing whatever you were doing. Was it just a hug, a fond avuncular hug? Or what? But, aside from all that, tell me what you think. You must think something analytic about those days. Why did he leave and what was I to do with his notes? Why was he so unhappy? Is there any historic figure with whom we can draw a parallel? Put it into another context for me, E., a nice, linear, algebraic equation, something leading to a definite yes or no. Tell me what you think. You have sources I have possibly neglected to study. You have a capacity to catch every detail and observe it thoughtfully. Tell me what went on back then, tell me what you know beneath your red hair."

Once both sides of the coaster had been covered with writing, I sat. The three-legged racing seemed to have stopped, my leash had been unclasped for the final mile of the journey, the aphrodisiac had brought about no love-driven fortitude and I have to admit that I needed to pull a trigger somewhere in my mind, fire a shot, to rouse myself from the Mai Tai Bar and the possibility that if I waited long enough, Miranda might walk in and change the afternoon for me.

Outside, the sun was still bright. I stood for a while, like a nocturnal, confounded by the colours and shapes of daytime. The watches and bags and shoes had an acutely original appearance, as did the hundreds of bamboo poles hanging with laundry from the apartment buildings. My eyes felt disconnected from the rest of me, as if images were being reflected without significance onto my retinas. I began to feel much the same as I had on the day of my arrival here, with everything fresh and without context and seeming to be such a precise and literal image of itself, with history and age present, yes, but stored out of view, beneath the earth and the concrete, bound together where they cannot be seen, like roots and pipes and the underground passageways Richard used to dream about.

Walk, walk, walk and I was across the street from the British Council where I found a bench and sat down. A man had set up a kiosk and was selling medallions bearing the names and faces of the saints. People stopped to look and the saints set up a pleasant clinking, like wind chimes, which soothed me while my eyes carried on with their separate existence.

It was then that Elizabeth came into view, across the street, her hair loose and in her hand a greasy bag of french fries which she picked at. Perhaps the aphrodisiac finally did have an effect, because at the sight of Elizabeth something came over me. Standing on the bench and cupping my hands in front of my mouth, I shouted "Elizabeth." She did not hear. "Elizabeth," I screamed louder. At that she stopped and saw me. I gestured for her to cross the street and she checked her watch, then darted across Nathan Road.

"Sit down," I said. "Sit down. Do you have much time?"

"Twenty minutes or so," she answered. "What are you doing here?"

"I was waiting for you," I said. My breathing was changing; I could feel my chest tightening as if there were a truss around my rib cage.

"Why would you wait for me here?" Elizabeth asked. There was a bit of ketchup on her upper lip and I wanted right then to hold her just for a moment, this cold fish of a cousin, give her some comfort, but I did not.

"I wanted to talk to you," I said. "I wanted to talk to you about Dad. That's why I came here in the first place, to Hong Kong."

Elizabeth's already pale face became a shade whiter. "Well, what? What about Duncan?"

"I can't think of a good way to ask this, except just to ask," I said, abandoning the coaster full of questions. There was a break in the traffic then, all that I was aware of was the tinkling of the medallions nearby. "What," I began, "what was there between you two? I saw you that last night from my bedroom. You were... hugging each other or something. I couldn't tell exactly. The image has been stuck in my mind for so long with no real explanation for it, and I have to know now, Elizabeth, what that was. I have to know."

"Gayle," Elizabeth said, standing up. "This is crazy. We're in the middle of Kowloon. We're in the street. I have to teach in twenty minutes. We can talk later."

"No," I said, pulling her by the arm back on to the bench. "No, we can't. It has to be now, Elizabeth. I took this potion, it's giving me extra courage," I added, trying to laugh.

Elizabeth stared at me for at least fifteen seconds. I thought she might cry, but she didn't. She had the look of someone watching a very tall building tumble to the ground.

"All right, Gayle. I'll tell you what was going on, as far as I know. As far as I know, there was nothing going on, the kind of nothing that's something. The kind of nothing that makes a person feel guilty for thirty or forty years.

"You could say it was like a flirtation, I guess, between a fifty-three-year-old uncle and his sixteen-year-old niece. Does that seem sick?" She did not wait for an answer. "Possibly, but at the time it didn't seem that way. It didn't seem that way at all. It didn't!

"You saw us that night? I should have known. I should have guessed that." Elizabeth paused for a moment, then went on. "I don't know. I don't know what to say. I've thought about it too and yet I can't come up with any answers either. He was lonely – he and Louise were so different. And he was probably even a little crazy. I don't know. He was unhappy and I was worried. That was the combination, I guess. That time I stayed at your house, those six months when Mom was sick, we used to talk, and if I told him to do something like milk the cows, he'd do it. I don't know why. He liked me. Then one day he confessed that he more than liked me, and it worried him. It worried him a lot. But nothing went on. Nothing. Your father wasn't screwing his niece, if that's what you're wondering. Until that last night and even then it was – well, he just held on to me for a while. And I didn't mind. It didn't seem creepy at the time – until the next day. I guess he knew he was leaving, he knew he was going to do himself in or whatever he did. So I admit to you that I liked him, too. I admit that to you Gayle. I liked Duncan a lot and I couldn't stop myself from liking him back then. But I don't blame myself for him leaving. I don't and I won't. That's all there is to it."

A blast of diesel exhaust hit my lungs, and I said, "So you're the longing that wouldn't end."

"The what?"

"The longing. It was on one of the notes."

With a tired sigh, Elizabeth said, "I honestly don't know. Maybe. But he had so many longings, it seemed. You should know that. Anyway, it was years ago and there simply is no way of knowing. There is no way of ever finding out, and people don't take kindly to that state of affairs. Or at least you don't."

There was a silence, and Elizabeth asked what it was I had taken, and when I told her, an aphrodisiac, we laughed. And when I described the clerk in the store and then May's reaction at the hotel, and the colour of it in my tea, we laughed some more. We laughed in the way that causes tears to spring forth from some place other than the tear ducts, that deep and ancient well, also near the eyes, where relief and sorrow are dissolved into one ambiguous element.

"I have to go," Elizabeth said. "I have to teach."

"But we need to talk about this more, don't you think?" I asked.

"Maybe," was her response, which from experience I know means unlikely, and she gave me a summary little kiss. Then she worked her way through the traffic to the British Council, up the stairs and through the revolving door. And the manner of her leaving, the manner of her disappearance behind that turning glass, reminded me of many things all at once; the caving in of earth as a plant is pulled from sandy soil, waves falling backward into themselves – flattened and hushed, the edges of a wound yielding to new skin. There will always be a smoothing over, a filling up, a burial; the measured sequels to change never fail us. Elizabeth has said what she could say, and I have heard, and already the sand is falling inward the way it does, with such order and precision.

The revolving door came to a halt. Time to go, I realized then. Time for this doubtful guest to head home. Or at least begin to head home.

What I've decided is to spend a month in Australia after I leave here; Miranda's parents will put me up. And early in October, maybe, return to Canada, and who knows what type of circumstance with Joel. In the meantime I will sit and watch the village come to life, wait for the sun to hit the white walls and the vines and the bougainvillea, and begin its silent work for another day.

Marion Douglas

The Doubtful Guests is Marion Douglas' first novel. Her short stories have been published in *The Journey Prize Anthology, Prism, Grain, Room of One's Own, Capilano Review* and *Prairie Journal of Canadian Literature*. She grew up in Ontario, never far from Lake Huron, and moved west in 1981. Ms. Douglas lives with her two children, Carla and Eric, in Calgary.

Other Orca Fiction Titles

THE LIONS	*Paul S. Sunga*
CROSSING THE LINE	*David H. Elias*
RAINCOAST MACABRE	*Philip Teece*
RAISE NO MEMORIAL	*William C. McConnell*
BREAKING THE CYCLE	*Maria Tippett*
THE PAGE TURNER	*Carol Wootton*